Seeing Red

NEWHEART COWBOYS 1

AISLING STORM

A. STORM INK

Contents

To those who feel different
you are always worthy of love.

Tropes & Triggers: Autism, bisexuality, bondage, cis-het romance, country-western romance, domination and submission (mild), degradation (mild), eating disorder (past) references, kidnapping, Neurodivergent affirming, second chances, small town vibes, social anxiety, suicide history reference

Chapter 1

Rose

Rose would never get used to these fancy shindigs. She'd rather be at home in her pajamas.

She stepped out of the limo, shivering in the early spring air. Dallas was warm most of the year, but not in February, and especially not after the sun went down.

Glancing up at the sparkling lights of The Pickett Center, the grand hall that had been selected for tonight's grant event, she shook out the dress Kitty had talked her into buying. The full-length, emerald satin gown was *gorgeous*. The high slit when she walked nearly went up to her panties, and the neckline almost down to her navel. The lady who helped her try it on had insisted the fancy wrap dress was secure and wouldn't come undone. She wasn't so sure, but the gorgeous green looked fantastic against her copper hair and pale, freckled complexion. And the expensive material was silky and luxurious against her skin, with no tags to scratch the back of her neck.

She had begged Kitty to come with her tonight. But while her best friend had driven into town to help Rose get ready, Kitty had her niece and nephew tonight and hadn't been able to get out of it. "Plus, those kinds of things are so stuffy," Kitty had said, scrunching her nose as she rolled her eyes while pinning Rose's hair.

You're telling me, Rose thought. She'd rather be at home curled up with a good book.

Thankfully it was early spring, and Rose didn't have to deal with the humidity tonight. Her hair had actually complied okay, at least. Her strawberry blond—okay, more strawberry than blond- hair had corkscrewed itself right up post-shower, thankfully not frizzing after she added her various creams to loosen the curl a bit. Kitty had helped her with her makeup. She had insisted Rose would have used way too little—and then proceeded to apply enough foundation that you almost couldn't see her freckles scattered across her nose and high cheekbones.

A gold dusting of shadow on her lids had enhanced her blue-green eyes, and the deep, dark liner Kitty had kept adding "just a little more" of made them pop. It was almost worth how long it would take to wash it all off at the end of the night. Kitty had also talked her into wearing lashes. Like, glue them onto your eyelids kind of lashes, which weren't as bad as she'd thought they would be, but still.

If one fell off into her soup tonight, she would die of embarrassment.

Of course, Kitty had made her wear her contacts, which Rose hated. But it was no use wearing the spidery lashes and hiding them behind glasses. With her thick curls twisted into a loose knot and a few tiny glistening gold hair pins tucked in where they were just noticeable in the sparkling lights, Rose almost looked fancy enough to be honored with a one hundred thousand dollar check.

She took a deep breath as she stepped into the crowded entrance hall along with the other recipients of the grant. This wasn't the first grant award she'd received, and it probably wouldn't be the last one she would apply for. There would never be enough funding for all the trauma research needed in the world, not unless some things on the planet began to change. Health markers were steadily worsening in a country where stress was high. Children were experiencing more and more trauma between rising cases of child abuse and neglect, school shootings, hunger, homelessness- the list went on and on.

Rose paused, focusing on her breath to stop the endless, helpless thought spiral that could so easily get out of control.

She was a graduate of the University of Texas, so to be a recipient of her alma mater's annual grant was important to her. As a neuroscientist, research was the heart of medical and educational advancement, and making the world a safer place just mattered to her. It mattered *so* much to her.

Rose checked herself in the gilded mirror just before entering the massive grand hall. *Everything seemed all in place,* she thought, as she turned and checked her profile. This neckline made her nervous. The sticky tape holding the silky material to her collarbones was all that stopped a nip slip. She wasn't even wearing a bra—thank god for good genes. There wasn't a bra in the world that wouldn't have shown with this gown. The tiny pale green lace thong she wore barely made it, but she refused to be completely underwearless, at least at this. She was a professional, goddammit.

The tiny sparkling diamonds in her ears had been a gift from her grandfather last Christmas. She felt her racing heart settle as she touched a fingertip to one.

"Go get 'em, Rosie," he would have said if he had seen her tonight. Her eyes glistened, but she swallowed the tears with another deep breath. Kitty would kill her if she ruined her makeup. There would be photographs for papers and websites at some point.

The ten grant recipients tonight were seated together, split between two tables, and Rose put the small, antique gold clutch she had borrowed from her grandmother in her seat. There wasn't much in there since it was ridiculously small, just her apartment key, her lipstick, and a fifty-dollar bill were she to get stranded. She hesitated to leave it there, but she needed to mingle. *Surely no one would see it tucked away beneath the chair at the table?*

Someone pressed a flute of champagne into her hand, congratulating her for securing the grant for her foundation. She pasted on a professional smile as flashes began to explode around her for various local and distant media enterprises.

She knew how to pretend to like this.

The event began with a reception, the guests mingling and the champagne flowing. She downed her first glass far too quickly through frequent small sips as she took quiet breaks from talking, hiding a bit when overwhelmed. She found herself being handed a second glass as another community member in another tuxedo jacket stepped up to ask more about her foundation.

"Well, if it isn't our beautiful Rosebud, all dressed up for a party and ready to shine!" She heard a familiar, laughing voice on the other side of the next flash. For the first time tonight, Rose genuinely smiled as she recognized Jackson Anderson. He had been the yearbook designer and editor of their school newspaper as well as the secretary for their senior class back at Newheart High. She'd heard he had been doing some reporting for the newspaper here in Dallas.

He flashed the camera one more time. "There's the money shot," he crowed, putting the camera down and swooping forward to kiss Rose on the cheek. "How ya doin' love?" he asked. "Kitty do your makeup? You look fantastic!" She saw him wink at the handsome photographer to her left. Rose's smile widened. Jackson hadn't changed a bit—always busy, always flirting, always knowing things.

"How'd you guess?" she asked, laughing. Kitty and Kendall, her sister, had the best little salon in Newheart, where they had all grown up together. "She actually drove up to help me get ready," she said, swishing her skirt one way and then the next, even doing a little twirl for his camera. Clearly, the bubbly was getting to her head, and she blushed a little. Jackson snapped another picture.

"That one should be in the grand return of The Newheart Gazette," Jackson told her, eyes never leaving the tall dreadlocked photographer as he moved on through the crowd. "Sorry, Rosebud, gotta go!" he barely got out as he twisted away, waving at her as he rushed in the same direction as the other camera guy.

"Wait!" she called, wanting to know more, trying to see through the crowd that had moved between them as he flitted off. The old paper hadn't been running in at least a decade. Interesting...

"He thinks he's going to restart the little hometown paper," a resolute voice said from behind her. She gulped and turned. A little deeper than she remembered, but she knew that voice without even looking at him.

"Hello, Red," Maxwell Anderson said, his eyes meeting hers and then slowly trailing down, down, down her impossible neckline. Then returning, up her long pale legs from those ridiculous four-inch gold heels Kitty had convinced her were perfect.

Rose swallowed again. It had been quite a long time since she'd seen him. Almost ten years in fact, since Max had nearly taken her virginity in the back of his brother's old Ford. The champagne was definitely going to her head. Otherwise, she wouldn't be remembering how they had steamed up the windows of the old truck before she had convinced him to join her on the blanket in that rusty truck bed.

"Rose Montgomery!" She heard Max's older brother Nat before she saw him walking up to his brother's side. Her eyes were still locked on Max's chocolate brown ones, like she was drowning in their molten lava, but Rose shook herself free and broke eye contact. She smiled shakily as she greeted Nathan Anderson, the oldest, largest, and kindest of the Anderson brothers.

"What are you guys doing here?" Rose asked, looking between them. She hadn't expected to see anyone from Newheart here. She spent more time in Dallas than she did Newheart anymore. The hour-and-a-half drive made it easy to be close to her family, but here in Dallas, she was close to work when she needed to go in, and the city had so much more to offer. Including space far from the handsome Anderson brothers—well, especially this one.

It had been a long time. She had tried to forget him.

"Well, you know our uncle is on the medical board over at the University of Texas Hospital," Nat reminded her, smiling jovially. "We often attend these things with him, but we especially were going to come when one of our own was being awarded!" Nat's rather large, burly self hugged her to his side for a moment and then released her kindly. Rose knew she gave awkward hugs at times.

Max remained silent, his eyes never leaving her. It made her so nervous, the intensity in his gaze. Her hands hadn't been shaking just a few moments ago when Jackson had been there, but she knew they were now.

"Oh," she said, remembering their connection to the hospital that was an offshoot of the University. She tried to smile around the lump in her throat. She took another sip of champagne to try to wash it down, the bubbly stuff spilling over the side of the cup a little as she sipped shakily.

"Dammit," she said. A dribble had gotten on the damn dress. She knew the shaking in her hand was ridiculously noticeable as she nervously wiped at the drip right above her breast with the cocktail napkin. She had to give a short speech and all after the damn meal. Could she not even handle a glass or two of champagne before then?

"Hey, I've got to catch up with the Oaklands. I saw them come in a few minutes ago," Nat said, looking at Max. "Max, you got her?" He glanced from Max to the trembling girl in the dribbled-on dress with a gentle look of pity.

Max sighed deeply. Rose heard it. Hey, she didn't need to be a bother to anyone. She was a big girl. She could take care of herself—she always had. She turned swiftly away, not even caring to say goodbye to Max, heading toward the ladies' bathroom she had seen when she arrived. But a firm grip on her elbow turned her in the opposite direction towards the bar instead.

The last thing she needed was another drink.

"A small glass of club soda, please." She heard Max ask the bartender quietly. The bartender took one look at her and then passed him a white bar towel as well. Max put a fifty-dollar bill in his tip jar.

Show off, she thought—but smiled gratefully to the bartender.

Steering her by the elbow again, he guided her outside the large room and down the corridor away from the crowded entry hall, where there was a quiet sitting area that no one seemed to have found yet. He stopped beside a large floor-length mirror and an empty bar counter and set down the glass tumbler.

Normally, Rose would have loved the break from the steady hum of the crowd, but now it just made her more anxious, being alone here with him. She swore she could hear her heart racing. Surely he could too.

"I could have taken care of it myself," Rose insisted impatiently, irritated that Max had just taken charge. His hand, still firmly at her elbow, brought goose bumps up and down her arms.

She remembered a time when she had longed for Max to touch her.

"And ruin that pretty dress with soap and water?" Max asked, an eyebrow sardonically raised at her. Rose thought he probably wasn't looking for an answer, so she pressed her lips together. Yes, she probably would have used soap and water in the ladies bathroom. Max dipped the tip of the bar towel into the club soda, pressing the excess out with his fingertips, and offered it to her. When she started to wipe at the stain, he sighed again deeply and quickly grabbed her wrist.

Taking the rag back, he said quietly, "Dab, Red, not wipe." And he gently pressed just the tip of the wet towel to the top of her breast, where the drink had spilled.

Rose swallowed again, barely breathing. He had to be able to hear her heartbeat. It was thundering so loudly in her ears. It wasn't her fault she hadn't been raised going to fancy parties like he and his brothers had. She hadn't worn very many fancy dress-up clothes to impress the Joneses. Deep down, she knew she wasn't being fair. The Anderson boys were good people, always had been. They weren't their money, but they did have its power.

She could feel the edge of his sleeve against her breast, the cold, hard cufflink lightly pressing its edge against her nipple. She wondered if he had realized it. Max's eyes rose from her breast to meet hers. He dabbed the dry side of the towel against her without even looking.

Unable to drop her gaze from his, Rose croaked, "Thanks, Max."

Max fisted the towel, their eyes still locked. He grazed his knuckles down over the soft satin and the tight bud that had become her nipple. Just once, for the briefest of moments. She swore her panties were instantly wet, just like on her sixteenth birthday.

He lowered his head, the towel in his hand at his side, his lips barely inches from hers. She could feel the brush of the crisp edges of his short beard against her chin and wondered what it would feel like against that nipple. Releasing a deep warm breath that fanned her cheek, he gently shook his head and stepped back, looking at her again.

"That should dry pretty quickly now," he said, his voice husky as he turned her by the elbow to face the mirror on the wall behind her.

Rose hardly saw the wet spot. But she did see the tall, dark, and handsome profile he made in his tuxedo behind her. His dark, wavy brown hair, with its expensive haircut, had grown longer from the short style he had worn as a teenager. The longer, dark brown curls now brushed his crisp white collar. His broad shoulders had only widened a bit more since his youth. She thought about how he had refused to play football his senior year as he had gotten involved in the student-led K-9 program at the local police station. She *still* remembered how angry her brother had said the coaches were with Max for "throwing away his sports career."

Standing tall behind her, his hand at her elbow, he met her gaze in the mirror. He had grown older for sure, but that had only made him more handsome.

She had heard he had spent some time in the Marines before taking a local job of some kind in Dallas, and she wondered what stories he shielded behind those dark and impenetrable eyes. The things he had seen and experienced. She wondered who he shared those stories with.

Rose swallowed, reminding herself to *breathe*. His eyes dropped to the movement of her throat and then her breasts in the mirror. The mirror didn't hide her response to him, nor did her dress. She'd probably need to take a walk for a few minutes to get her nipples to settle themselves down and her panties a little less hot before sitting in this damn dress.

She slipped out from in front of him and began to back away in the other direction.

"I really should go. Thank you, though." Remembering his deep sighs earlier, she added, "I really didn't mean to be a bother."

She spun and walked quickly away, the dress spinning behind her, her long bare legs flying as quickly as she could in those ridiculous heels to get away from him without breaking into a run.

Finally, Rose reached the front doors. Pushing through them, she sagged against the wall to the side of the entrance for a moment, gasping in the fresh air. The night air was cool, and she desperately needed cool. Sweat had begun to glisten at her temples.

Goddamnit Max. He had fucked up her whole junior and senior years, and now this. She could still pull off the speech. The spot on the dress seemed almost dry, barely noticeable. She would just have to not look in his direction, or she might not be able to keep her thoughts straight—just like the last few moments had been. She wasn't even certain of the time and knew she needed to get back in, having left her watch off with tonight's dress.

Taking one final breath, she opened the door.

"Shoulders back, Rosie girl," she heard her grandfather say again.

You can do this.

Max

Max had known she would be here, his rosebud of the night. But he hadn't expected the one-two punch to his gut when he saw her. She had to be around 27 now, two years his junior, but the last time he had seen her, she had been a blossoming 16. He still remembered her soft pink lips wrapped around him in his brother's old Ford, those seafoam green, mermaid eyes peering widely up at him, daring him to swim in their depths. That night had been a mistake, even for a randy almost 18-year-old.

He'd expected her not to affect him as much this time around. *He'd calculated that wrong.*

He sat at the family table as the event shifted into the meal portion of the night. The chilled soup did little to cool his libido as he remembered her reflection in that long-gilded mirror. Her legs were ridiculously long in those damn heels and that impossible neckline. Dear God, he had swung rapidly from wanting to pull it tightly together so no one would fantasize about her as he had through the years, to wanting to peel it completely back onto her shoulders, exposing those damn nipples that had hardened the moment she saw him, photographers be damned. His fingers had itched to touch her, but just as he had as a goddamned teenager—damned if he did and damned if he didn't—he chose not to.

His best friend's little sister was off-limits.

Even if the blond cheerleader he'd fucked many times behind the bleachers in high school heard him slip Rose's name a few times. Laurel hadn't deserved that, and he'd told her as much when he left and enlisted just after graduation. He knew if he hadn't gotten his ass outta Dodge, he would have lost control, and then he'd fuck everything up for her.

The dinner entree came, and Max had chosen the expensive cut of beef that he knew came from the Anderson Brothers line. The food did little to distract him, and neither did the conversation that flowed at the table. His brothers and his parents chatted as they caught up with their Uncle, whom they rarely saw, but Max had just had lunch with him last week. Instead, Max still saw her sixteen-year-old sunlit gaze of strawberry wine-induced confidence as she asked him to take her to Moonlit Point. He'd lasted a full year of having recognized her adoring gaze for what it was. Oh, that youthful cock-that-wouldn't-quit, with the countless times he'd rubbed one out in the shower over her. He'd fucking caved after holding back nearly long enough to make it to graduation and get away from their small hometown.

Max watched as, one at a time, the recipients of the neurological program awards began to be addressed. He'd felt her presence over at her table on the other side of the room, but his view had been blocked by the many attendees at the event. *All for the better.* Clearly, his own discipline was lagging tonight. He wasn't that impulsive teenager anymore when he'd grazed her aroused nipple like that.

Matt would still knock him out if he knew how lustful his thoughts ran towards Matt's sister.

Over the ten or so years since graduating, he'd stayed connected to his closest friend, making sure that Matt's sister wasn't around when they caught up. He knew she'd successfully completed her degrees in biology and neuroscience, starting the research foundation that meant so much to her. He hadn't expected less. Growing up, she had always had her nose in a book, her freckled cheeks hidden more often than not by her curls or a biography of some kind. She'd rather read than think about her father's death, just as much as Matthew had jumped headfirst into getting the shit kicked out of him by the bullies at school as the new kid. Until the Anderson brothers had stepped in.

You just didn't mess with an Anderson brother. There was generally one around when you needed them. And they looked out for the people they cared about.

Nat, nicknamed after their grandfather, was the fairly typical oldest brother, always caring about everyone's welfare. He was big at 6'6", and had quickly advanced on the wrestling team at school. He knew how to fight, although ironically didn't like to, as he was the peacekeeper of the bunch.

Max was the middle kid and had swapped places, it seemed, with Nat for controlling the lot of them rather than peacekeeping like the typical middle child. As a kid, he often got anxious when things weren't in order and often sought to control his environment around him. So as an adult, he eventually swapped controlling things for people with the acceptable military discipline he took on. He had attended therapy for a bit as a young adult and learned about how his brain worked. He'd learned to adjust some of his compulsions, incorporating mindful meditation and other cognitive tools to keep his need to control within appropriate measures.

Jackson, the youngest, had a way with words and had learned to use them to get what he wanted. So, if it wasn't Jackson starting shit, or Max's need for control, then Nat's natural size seemed to put people naturally on the defensive with them. But no matter what, they all came to the aid of the other.

That was brotherhood.

That was being an Anderson.

Chapter 2

Max

Finally, his uncle stepped up to the podium. With great Newheart pride, he introduced Rose. Having been friends with her father in childhood, he spoke to her skills, time at the University, and the work her foundation had already begun in educating the world on the outcomes of trauma.

Rose accepted the funding graciously, of course, with her practiced smile. "For a lifetime, I have faced the outcomes of how trauma impacts the developing brain. When my father died when I was young, it was unimaginable how impactful the loss might be for all of us. Today we are coming to understand the various health markers that can be—"

Max felt the rumble and was moving before the blast fully shook the room.

The explosion deafened him, the sound of wood splintering terrifyingly as he wasn't sure he could get to her fast enough. He flashed on his time in the Middle East and protecting his military family. He hadn't even thought before moving.

He just knew Rose was at ground zero, and he could not leave her behind.

The lighting and speakers, the various rigging overhead, began to creak, warning they were likely coming down. His uncle had been thrown from the front of the stage, but Nat and his father were already moving towards him.

Reaching the stage, he saw she had been thrown towards the back, the massive background now in pieces but miraculously standing. Her head was tilted limply as she slumped against the back wall, a trickle of blood running down the wall behind her.

"Fuck, Red," he mumbled. He wrapped his fingers around her wrist, his thumb at her pulse, which was soft and erratic. *She better be okay, or I'll fuck someone up.*

Hell, he probably would anyways.

His attention homed in as he checked the immediate area, knowing he had to get her off that stage in case further damage occurred. Picking her up, her dress dangling over his arm, torn at her shoulder, but thankfully still barely keeping her decent for now. He tucked her head against his shoulder, elbowing his way past the stage help who were scrambling to know if everyone was okay. The crowd was in an uproar behind him, but he had no time or thought for the others. Moving quickly, he carried her down the dark back hallway, alert to any movements in the shadows, armed should he need to defend them.

He was thankful now that he had gone through the extra steps to get through security with his badge and gun rather than leaving them at home.

He reached the empty green room down the hall, laying Rose down carefully on the couch. He gently checked the back of her head where the blood was, noting the small gash was clean, so he pressed the handkerchief from his pocket against it tightly. She moaned but didn't wake.

He sent a quick voice chat to his brothers in their message thread, letting them know where he was. He requested an update, stat, and an EMT. Nat responded that the police had arrived quickly and were emptying the massive auditorium, bringing in the K-9 units to sweep, and that family was okay. Their Uncle had a gash on his forehead but otherwise would be fine, and Nat was sending an EMT their way.

Jackson eventually responded that the explosion seemed to have been a small pipe bomb set up underneath the stage in a floor vent, small and acrid but not likely intended to cause severe harm.

Only to frighten, Max thought.

Someone was sending a message.

Rose

Rose woke up in the emergency bay to the sound of Max telling the nurse he wasn't leaving her.

"No, I'm *not* her family," he said, his voice like ice. "But just try to make me leave," he told the woman. His uncle's calm voice followed, soothing the angry nurse as their voices moved further away.

Rose groaned, trying to open her eyes, but they were *so heavy.* They fluttered a bit, the lights behind her lids so excruciatingly bright. She felt him move closer to her, felt his hand on hers.

His voice gentled, "Your mother is on her way, but it will be a little while yet. I got you, Red. Rest."

Maybe I could for just a few minutes more...

Rose

What must have been more than a few minutes later, because her mother was sitting next to her hospital bed crocheting, Rose opened her eyes, trying again.

"Ohhhh myyyy goddddd..." Her head ached.

"They said they gave you something for that a little while ago," her Momma said softly. "A mild concussion, baby, but you'll be okay." She grasped Rose's hand, her eyes tearing. "I'm so glad you're okay, darlin'."

Her mother reached over and muted the already quiet tv, pressing the nurse's button. Caroline Montgomery had thrown a few things in a bag and, despite being thrown together, still carried herself as classy as ever. Her shoulder-length blond curls had long gone gray but were pulled back in a hair clip.

"They said to alert them if you woke," she explained as she turned on a light beside Rose's bedside.

A nurse rushed into the room, checking the numbers on the various cords and machines they had attached to her. Max walked in behind her, and Rose's eyes widened. She had to look like shit. I mean, she was in a hospital gown. *Who changed her into the damn hospital gown?*

Her eyes darted around wildly, her pulse rate rising and setting off the machines.

"Don't worry, Princess Rosebud," he said, guessing at her stress. "Your virtue is intact. The nurses handled everything."

"Don't call me that," she heard herself say a bit petulantly. *A bit adolescently*, she reminded herself. *Girl, you have a doctorate in how the brain works.*

He winked at her. "Glad you are awake," he said, his hand coming to rest on the side of her face, tilting her eyes up to meet his. He nodded his head after what looked like checking her pupils.

Why was he wearing a holstered gun?

Again, he seemed to read her confusion right. "Sorry, Red. My jacket got a little dirty tonight." He flipped open his badge. "I actually work here in Dallas in the K-9 unit, so they've let me in on a little bit of the info as they've gathered it." He addressed both her and her Mom. "So tonight, there was a small pipe bomb set in a rear floor vent under the back of the stage. There have been no fingerprints, no traces of clues of any kind, which makes me think this wasn't an amateur, but it's strangely small for a pro, so I think it was a message of some kind. Only, we don't know who for or why."

"Yet, anyways," he added, sitting on the edge of the bed, his thumb sliding along hers. The monitors pinged as her oxygen monitor dropped a bit and her heart rate elevated. Dammit. Why must she be attached to machines that gave her away so easily? Rose blushed.

Max winked at her again but shifted off the bed, giving her space. "I have a proposal."

Jackson walked in, followed by a rather large German Shepherd on a leash. "Well, that escalated quickly," he said, laughing at his own joke. "I thought you just wanted her to move in?" The Shepherd came directly to Max and sat quietly as Jackson passed off the leash. The large, quiet dog seemed to be waiting for something.

"Wait—what?!" Rose startled, her eyes flying to Max from the well-natured dog, no longer thinking about snuggling him, er—the dog that is.

"Now, Rose..." her mother began, "it will only be for a little while."

"Y'all talked about this already?" Rose's voice began to rise. Ow, that hurt. She winced and brought her voice back down to just above a whisper. "Without even consulting me?"

Jackson sat back in his chair, plopping his black boot on his knee. "I mean, Rosie, you were fairly unavailable to discuss it, being unconscious and all," he smiled widely at her, teasing.

I mean, he wasn't wrong. Still, they should have asked her.

"Why?" Rose asked simply. "You don't know if it had anything to do with me. And I have work to do here in Dallas."

"Which was why I thought it the best solution since Max lives here in Dallas," her mother said. "Obviously, coming home would be even better, but are you going to agree to that?" she asked with a raised eyebrow, already knowing the answer.

Why was her mother betraying her? Oh, right, 'cause no one had a clue she almost fucked Max once upon a time, and now it was all awkward as hell. Well, Kitty knew some, but definitely not the currently awkward part.

But her mother was right about one thing. "Nope, not staying in Newheart," she said flatly. She didn't mind visiting, but long-term? She'd gotten outta Dodge when she could. That quaint little happy town had too many memories in it.

"So, you'll stay with me," Max said quietly, "and Buck here." The dog tipped his head at her inquisitively. "Just for a little while until we know more."

"But... I have Luna," she said hesitantly.

"That's her new kitten," her mother jumped in. "Really a sweet little thing, sometimes."

"Sometimes?" laughed Jackson. "I wanna meet this sometimes sweet kitten," he joked.

"Should make for a fine bunkmate, Buck," Jax said to his brother's dog as he got up. "Okay, Nat grabbed the things you requested from your car, big brother. I'm out," he said, kissing Rose's cheek gently. "I hope they gave you good drugs for the headache you're fittin'ta have," he teased as he walked out.

Nat walked in, handing a small bag to Max, talking low for a moment. Turning to Rose, he took her hand between his two big ones. "Don't you worry a bit about your Momma. We have her taken care of tonight, staying in one of our secure apartments in the city. We'll make sure she gets home nice and safe, don't you worry, darlin'." Nat always did take care of everything.

Her mom kissed her cheeks, saying how thankful she was that the Anderson boys had been by her side. Rose blushed a bit again—if only her mother knew. Nat and her Mom soon headed out for the night, as it was late, and she wanted to rest.

Rose yawned.

"They were talking about releasing you tonight, Red. You wanna kick this joint?" Max asked calmly. She wasn't sure, but he may have been giving her a way out for the night. But like hell was she staying here all caught up in these cords and beeps that gave away her secrets.

"Do I get my dress back?" she asked, a bit annoyed at being naked under the stiff hospital gown that was wide open in the back. The dress covered her more if you took the back into consideration. Plus, it cost way too much to leave behind.

"Well, the dress didn't quite make it through the ambulance ride." His eyes twinkled. Dammit. She probably didn't want to know that story. That dress cost more than she liked to remember.

Max set the small duffle bag his brother had brought him on the bed. "It's not much, but there are some clothes in here that will make do until we can get some of your things."

He gently tapped the side of his thigh, and his pup got up, alert, and walked toward the door. Turning back, he looked at her, his eyes a little too honest. "I don't bite, Red. Not unless you want me to."

Their eyes held for a moment, and he was out the door.

Max

Whyyyyyyy? Max groaned to himself.

Why did he say that?

'Unless you want me to,' did not pass muster, at least not with Max. Rose wasn't fling material. She wasn't someone he could sleep with a few times while they shacked up over an investigation and then never think about again.

Sure, he had no doubt in his mind that it would be good between them. Their interaction over her dress alone told him that. *The past told him that too*, the guilty voice in his head whispered.

But an unconscious Red had scared the shit outta him.

The fact that he still cared this much scared the shit outta him.

Hell, he still remembered her little 6-year-old freckled cheeks and angry frown when she spit on him after he tugged her wild, curly pigtails the day he had met Matt. He'd watched her grow up from there, almost two years and two grades behind him and her brother, as she often raced behind them, wanting to be included. Until she hadn't. She'd met Kitty early on, and when the teen years hit, she started hanging more with her than her brother and him. They'd do nails or some other feminine thing all the time, or she'd have her nose stuck in a book. And he'd missed her chasing after them, telling them they had to include her. She had actually been smarter than Matt and his friends despite being two years their junior. He'd always wanted her on his team—even the rough games, cause what she couldn't maneuver physically, she'd understood tactically.

He'd missed her. And then she'd grown tits, and those cherry pink heart lips, and that had changed everything for him.

Tonight, touching her had consumed him if only for a few moments, not knowing that only an hour or so later, he would be shielding her unconscious body with his jacket when her dress fully ripped on an ambulance ride to the hospital. He'd known her pulse was steady enough but had been uncertain as to how her head was.

She hadn't woken up—not even once after being thrown. He had been in goddamned warfare before, and yet he had never been so afraid in all of his life. He had willed her to open her eyes, but she had remained still, lifeless.

The nurse came out of her room, mentioning the doctor had called in a prescription for some painkillers if they wanted to stop and get them from the pharmacy at the end of the corridor before leaving. Rose needed to be woken at least every few hours to monitor her concussion. Between active duty and his training as a police officer and detective, he had no doubts that he could follow the aftercare protocol just fine.

When she stood in the doorway—in his clean workout shirt that did little to hide her braless breasts and the drawstring pants, which she had pulled tight and folded at the ankle for length—he wondered if this might be a life test he might not pass. He swallowed around the lump in his throat, then went to help her, knowing she was likely light-headed. She'd refused a wheelchair, but she didn't refuse to lean on his arm—he suspected she regretted refusing the wheelchair but was too stubborn to admit it.

They stopped at the pharmacy to grab the script on the way out, Buck trotting by his side. When she stumbled just outside the door, he ignored her protests as he swung her up in his arms again, carrying her the rest of the way to his black Explorer, giving his usual low bird whistle when Buck got distracted by the dumpster.

He set her carefully in the passenger seat, putting his finger to her lips when she protested again. "Stop. I'll take care of you." But he suspected it was the touch that actually shut her up. For now, he'd take it. She needed to rest and accept help.

He let Buck into the back and then sat behind the wheel for a moment before asking her. "Do you want to get some things from your place tonight or wait until tomorrow?"

She thought for a moment. "Tonight, if you don't mind," she said quietly. "I'd rather not leave Luna on her own. She's too little. I just found her in the alley last week." She looked at him with pleading eyes. She didn't need to, he wasn't an asshole to leave a kitten alone all night. But God, those eyes. He swore they were mermaid sirens.

"Would you rather direct me or give me the address?" he asked her quietly, holding out his phone. He'd known they were both in Dallas for the last two years together. Matt had mentioned it a few times. But he'd always been careful not to ask any questions that would give him insight into where she lived and avoided any temptation to find her. Thankfully, they'd just never crossed paths in the large city.

She added her contact information in the phone with an address in Arlington, mentioning it was just south of the college campus, as she taught two classes in addition to her research work there. Ironic as he lived not far from there. He'd chosen a secure condominium in east Arlington as it wasn't too far from the Marine base in West Dallas when he had returned stateside. He clicked the address and pulled up the map.

She laid her head back against the seat as he drove in silence, letting her rest, but when he got close, she directed him to a small, secure lot behind a row of quaint shops and a coffeehouse. He helped her down from her seat after she insisted on walking. He quietly told Buck to stay, and he followed her into the dark alley, his senses fully alert. Without his jacket, his holster was fully visible, so he knew the likelihood of anyone surprising them was low. Still, after the unexpected night they'd had, his instincts were on high alert. At least the parking area had been secured by an electronic gate with a passcode that she'd told him as he'd entered. They went up the barely lit stairwell and entered her second-floor apartment, greeted almost immediately by a small gray kitten with a white patch around her eye. He immediately bent down and scratched the mewling baby's forehead as she rubbed against his pant leg.

"Of course, she'd love you," she said, rolling her eyes, then squinted as she touched her temple regretfully. "I'll just get a few things. Hold on."

He tucked away his response to her rolled eyes and picked up the little kitten, who immediately began rubbing against his chin, currently thickened with dark scruff. He sat on her vintage green couch in her small open living area. He'd remained clean-shaven daily for Marine life but had grown lax with his detective work in the local city department. The scruffy, short beard made him a little easier to talk to most of the time, softening his approach on the street when needed.

Her space was comfortable, filled with some antique furniture pieces that represented her style and were likely worth a pretty penny. Softened with candles, throw blankets, and magazines, along with a few small cat toys. One full wall housed a built-in bookshelf overflowing with books of all kinds from research to smutty romances. He had noticed the alarm near the door that she'd turned off when she arrived home, noted the company and the basic number she'd used to turn it off, and added it to his list. He needed to convince her to upgrade before she returned home.

The place was small but open concept, with a corner kitchen with vintage-style, smaller red appliances. He noted no dishwasher, but there was a small triangular island, and the corner over the sink was all windows facing the cross street. Another window was further down the wall, overlooking a small vintage table and two chairs. Again, a security concern he would need to address. She needed blinds at a minimum, rather than the wide open, sheer curtains at the ends for decoration. An unbidden thought of her walking around naked except for her glasses after dark flitted through his mind before he pushed it away.

She came out of the bedroom at the back with a carry-on bag. She set the leather bag on the small kitchen table, grabbed a soft reusable bag of some kind, and began to gather items for the kitten.

"You don't have a cat, right?" she looked at him inquisitively. When he shook his head, she began to collect the items needed for the kitten's litter.

"Come, Luna," she cooed to the small kitten as she took her from his lap, her fingertips grazing his thigh where the kitten had settled and was purring. He felt himself stir but ignored his body as he stood. Red put the tiny kitten into the small, ventilated carrier bag she had pulled out. "Thankfully, I got this when I took her to the vet after I found her last week."

She stood back and looked around. She'd added a laptop bag to the table as well. "I actually don't go into the University very often right now. My two classes are virtual, so hopefully, you have a space I teach from?" she asked, looking at him uncertainly."

He told her about his office/guest room and how it would likely meet her needs just fine. He worked from there at times but could work just fine from the couch or dining room table. He kept the sofa bed in there for when friends or family came in and didn't want to stay on their own. More often than not, family stayed in one of the other secure units they had in the city, but friends wanted to be close, to catch up.

He shouldered her bags from the table and picked up the litter items. She set the alarm and locked the unit behind them, grabbing her mail on the way out and shoving it in the side pocket of her laptop bag that he carried. She gingerly made her way down the steps with the kitten, and he watched her carefully in case she fell.

Not that he would have admitted that out loud. She would have told him she didn't need him to, but her steps were still shaky.

There was light traffic with it being so late, so it only took about fifteen minutes to reach his gated condominium community from her apartment. He scanned the fob to get past the gates and wound his way past the pool and tennis courts to his building unit. He pressed the button on the Explorer for the private garage door.

"Nice," Rose said, "A garage... Must be nice when it rains." She touched her hair self-consciously. He'd always thought no one had hair like Rose did. It was like flames in its various ginger shades. The corkscrew curls would wrap themselves around your finger. Well, he'd always pretended to pull her hair when he'd wrap them around his fingers.

He checked his mirrors before getting out of the car. He let Buck out next, who circled the car and then went to wait patiently by the door. He grabbed her things, and by the time he got around to her door, she'd already gotten out of the car and stood waiting for him, struggling to meet his eyes, uncertain.

He knew the feeling, even if he hid it better.

He turned the house alarm off from his key ring in his pocket with his thumbprint, then unlocked both deadbolt locks. He gestured for her to go after Buck, so he could follow up the flight of stairs as the unit was over the garage. He secured the locks, including the additional internal third lock, and then made his way up the stairs behind her. While his clothing practically hung on her, her ass was still as fine as it had been all those years before. Again, he felt himself stir and fully ignored it.

The stairs opened into the back laundry, where he set her bags for the moment. He reset the alarm to occupied, allowing for internal movement. He showed her where he'd suggest the litter box be, under the laundry sink, as the laundry door was usually open. She agreed, so he opened the bag she'd put it in and took it out. Rose let out Luna and introduced it to her.

The tiny kitten pawed at her sand and christened it, and then proceeded to explore the rest of her new space.

He moved on and turned on some lights. He knew his condo was bigger than the average apartment. He really didn't need all the space, but his mother had convinced him that he wanted a space big enough for his first family, were he to share it with anyone. He hadn't had plans for any of that but thought it would save him a move one day. Plus, he liked the pool, and their smallest unit was this two-bedroom.

His mom had hired a decorator eventually when after three months, all he had in the place was his bed and his elliptical. It wasn't fancy, but it wasn't bare bones anymore, either. Buck appreciated his soft dog bed, which he'd claimed now.

Buck looked woefully at Max as the tiny kitten had found his tail.

"Be good," he said firmly. But Max knew he would be. Buck was fantastically patient, far more than Max was some days. That's how they got their work done, methodically seeking answers and finding truths.

He gave her a brief tour of the open-concept dining area with the six chairs that he literally never sat in. The living area with a fireplace and a big flatscreen television over it with a couch and an armchair. Then the open kitchen with an island and stools separated it from the living area. Down the short hall was the full bath, second bedroom with office and sofa bed, and then his room. He mentioned he had his own bathroom, and she could have the main one all to herself.

He saw her stumble a bit and told her she should sit down for a while, while he got things set up for her in the office. He obviously hadn't been prepared for her. She tried to argue, but when he pressed her shoulder into the chair, she didn't resist too well. She definitely looked tired. He popped the leg of the armchair up, and Luna jumped up almost immediately to snuggle at her legs.

"See," he said. "Even Luna agrees." And did his best not to touch her. He'd wanted to tweak her chin or tuck her loose curl behind her ear but knew it wasn't in their best interest. Instead, he turned on the tv and handed her the remote, showing her how to find the guide and change the channels.

He set out towels in the extra bathroom, thankful the cleaning lady had come the day before. He pulled out the sofa bed. His brother had assured him it had been a decent sleep when he stayed there for a few weeks before getting his own condo unit in the same community. Jackson stayed in Dallas generally, working for the Dallas Morning News and traveling at times for them, despite planning to eventually go back to Newheart to reform the old town paper. Nat lived back home in a small cabin on their land, running the old family ranch with their father. When he came into town for the Anderson offices, he swapped staying with each brother to catch up.

He added clean sheets to the sofa bed, the thick-down comforter his mother had picked up for him, and a few pillows. He opened the closet so she would see that one side was empty with storage space and empty hangers for clothing, despite the other side holding various office items and boxes.

There was still plenty of room to walk around the sofa bed, and one wall was floor-to-ceiling built-in bookshelves he'd built himself and painted white to match the walls. The wall the door was on held the antique walnut desk with a roll top that had been his grandfather's. Over the desk was his whiteboard, where he had a few cases going, organizing his thoughts and facts, but he didn't bring much home that was confidential. If he did, that generally remained in his messenger bag. To the side of the desk was an old four-drawer walnut file cabinet he'd found at an estate sale to match the desk. Jackson had nearly killed him when he had to help Max move it—it was so heavy.

He'd need to make sure she didn't face the camera towards his evidence board when she taught, but he figured she'd be sitting at the desk anyways, as he usually did.

He knew it was past 2am at this point, so he went back to get her things and saw she had fallen asleep in the chair with it tipped back, the kitten sleeping at her shoulder. He brought her things to the room first, placing her laptop bag on the desk chair, and her other bags against the wall for her to do with as she liked.

Back in the living room, he hunched down and gently touched her cheek.

"Red," he said softly, it was a punch to the gut when her soft lashes fluttered open, and she looked at him. Time spun backward as he remembered that trusting look in an old truck bed long ago.

"Let's get you to bed, little one," he said now instead.

"Who you callin' little, Max?" she grumbled, gathering the kitten from her shoulder. She tried to pull the chair release for the legs to go down but fumbled.

"That would be you, Red," he said. "But I got ya..."

He tilted the release forward, his hand at her back to help her rise. His t-shirt on her braless breasts had tempted him all night and now was no different as she brushed by him, the soft, worn-out t-shirt not doing much to hide her pebbled nipples against his arm.

He swallowed a groan and knew he'd probably need a cold shower tonight.

He followed her to the office door just to make sure she made it all right, but when they got there, she turned and stood up on her tiptoes and surprisingly kissed his cheek. Her hardened tits pressed against his forearms, folded at his chest.

"You're not comin' in," she slurred sleepily, the pain medication talking, he was sure. "Not by the hair of my chinny chin, chin."

She turned and stripped off his pants as she climbed into the bed. He felt himself stiffen since he knew she didn't have a stitch on underneath. He'd seen them strip her of the torn garment at the hospital when he'd refused to leave. He had needed to make sure she would be okay—he owed Matthew, her brother, that much.

Who was he kidding? *He'd* needed to know she would be okay.

"I gotta check on you in a few hours Red," he called from the door as he turned off her light, already planning that cold shower.

"You can try..." she challenged him, even though she was already half asleep.

Dear God, how was he going to survive this?

Chapter 3

Red

“Hey... Red.” She heard for the third time. He needed to leave her alone. It was still dark out.

She felt the bed beside her settle as someone sat down. *What the hell was Matt doing in her room?* “G’away,” she mumbled, turning over in the bed, a leg flipping the covers out of the way as she pulled the pillow over her head. Her pounding head.

She felt a hand at her waist, another attempt at pulling the pillow out from over her. Wait, the name they used registered—Matt didn’t call her Red.

She peeked around the pillow edge. The light from the hallway was behind him, but it was definitely not Matt. She pulled the pillow back over her head as she remembered. “No, really, go away,” she said more clearly this time.

He chuckled. "I have painkillers."

She slowly removed the pillow and saw his offered hand. She knew her hair would be a fright. She realized she'd kicked off the blanket, and the t-shirt barely went past her pantiless state. Barely. She flipped the edge of the blanket back over her lap.

He held out the glass of water and two pills to her.

"I will take them, but this does not mean I like being woken up," she said grumpily.

"Duly noted," he said, his hand coming up to cup the side of her face after she took the pills. She realized he was checking her pupils. He tucked a tendril of her hair behind her ear.

"God," she said, running her hand over her hair and pulling it down around her ears, knowing it must be wild since she hadn't secured it before sleeping. "Don't mind me. You can go back to sleep now," she grumbled, turning over onto her belly and pulling the soft pillow back over her head. She felt the coolness on her ass cheeks and hoped he didn't notice in the dark.

SLAP. She jumped— Nope, he'd noticed. "Dammit, Max, GET OUT!" She threw the pillow, barely hitting the door as he slipped out. Too tired to get up and get it, she grabbed the other pillow and turned over, grumbling about brothers and their friends as she slipped back into sleep, trying to forget the feel of his fingertips brushing her labia when they had smacked her ass.

He woke her once more before he finally just let her sleep in until she eventually woke with the sun high in the sky. The door to the office was cracked open, and she wondered where Luna had gone. She did, however, add a bra and normal-ass panties under the sweatpants before she went looking. And a ponytail for her wild curls.

She found the kitten curled up against Buck on his dog bed, which was the absolute cutest thing. She scratched Buck's ears and told him so. She didn't see Max and his bedroom door was closed, but she did smell coffee, so she investigated. She found cream in the large commercial fridge, wondering why he needed something so big for just himself. But then maybe it wasn't just him, she thought, having never considered he might have someone in the bedroom with him, someone who maybe even lived with him. She nervously fluttered her hands around, suddenly overwhelmed with what to do next.

That would be horribly awkward. Her fingertips fluttered weakly again in the air.

I mean, it wasn't like she was still in love with Max or anything like she had been as an awkward teen. Just because he made her stomach do all kinds of fluttery ass stuff, and she couldn't think straight when he was around— which was highly irregular for her, as she greatly depended on her intelligence—didn't mean she was still in love with him. That had just been a teenage crush. A rough one, remembering how much she had struggled with depression her junior year after he left town and enlisted.

The year after he hadn't wanted her.

She wasn't ever going back there again. It had taken her the following senior year to dig her way out of the hell hole she'd sunk into.

She started to think about how quickly she could gather her things and get out of there before whomever he was with came out of that bedroom. She could see it now... poor Rose, always had a crush on Max, and here he was, having to look after her again.

She heard the bedroom door open and began to panic more, freezing in place.

But he came around the corner to the kitchen with a towel around his neck, sweat dripping, and wearing a pair of running shorts sans a shirt. Alone. He reached into the fridge and took out the orange juice, pouring a small glass, his head nodding to whatever music was in his AirPods. He jumped a bit when he saw Rose on the other side of the island.

"Shit, Red," he said, pulling out an earbud. "I didn't see you there." He used his towel to mop his face and looked at her again. "You all right?" he asked cautiously.

"Yeah, um," she began hesitantly. "I just was... startled... too, I guess." *Did you get married? Got a live-in partner? I don't want to be in the way of anyone,* she thought anxiously.

But she kept her mouth shut.

He leaned against the opposite counter and studied her. "What is it really?" he asked quietly. It was that quiet voice— he had always gotten her to say things she didn't want to say. Well, she did want to, but was just too nervous.

"I'm— I'm—" she swallowed to clear her throat with how naked he was. "I'm not in anyone's way staying here, right?" she asked hesitantly, dropping her eyes to her toes to avoid his chest.

"Red," he said firmly, waiting until she looked up at him. "I live alone. I'm not seeing anyone right now. If I were, I'd tell you, I promise." But he kept looking at her for a minute.

"Are you seeing anyone right now?" he asked directly. She shook her head no, not breaking eye contact.

Rose didn't always make eye contact as easily as others. Social anxiety ensured that— no matter how much she practiced, or her coach gave her tips. But somehow, with Max, it had always been exciting. Intense. Even her junior year, that last year he had been around, they would catch eye contact from across the lunchroom, Rose had thought. Or maybe he had just been looking at some girl behind her. He'd always had a cheerleader with him of some kind, even after he had quit the team.

She awkwardly dropped her eyes, looking at her coffee and taking a sip as she tried to slide past him. He stopped her with a hand on her arm.

"As long as you're here, treat this like home, okay?" he asked her when she met his eyes again. "Just like your Momma would tell me when I'd come over with Matt."

She smiled softly at him and nodded, moving into the living area and sitting cross-legged in the corner of the couch. Luna came over to investigate and sniffed at her pant leg, playing with a loose string. Max set the remote by her and mentioned he was going to jump in the shower.

"There are towels in the extra bathroom if and when you need them," he said.

He just needed to move on with his shirtless self so she could get her head back on straight. Those shoulders. Those abs. Damnit. She was definitely not an exerciser. He clearly was.

Dear god, 24 hours ago, she would have never in a million years imagined where she was right now. Literally anywhere other than Maxwell Anderson's couch. How was she supposed to wrap her head around what to do with all this when she could have never imagined it in the first place?

She wondered how long she would be here.

Luna had curled back up with Buck, who was being a dutiful guardian. So, Rose decided to take a shower as well. She hadn't washed all that makeup off her face last night and had noticed some of it on the pillowcase this morning. She'd have to replace that if she couldn't get it to wash off the pretty embroidery-edged pillowcase. She bet his Momma picked those out.

She took her toiletry bag into the bathroom and sorted some of her stuff, putting a few items in the shower and some on the counter. It was a shower only, no bath, but it was beautifully tiled with different shades of teal and blue pebbles, designed to look like a river from the top corner down to the drain in a sea of white tile. The rain-style shower head was fantastic, although she was careful when washing her hair where she had hit her head as it was tender. The ER Doctor had assured her the waterproof glue stitches would release on their own in good time, but she would follow up with her doctor in a few weeks.

She pulled back the loose white double-layered curtain after she was finished, wrapping her hair in one thick fluffy white towel and her body in another as she stepped out into the steam. She applied eye and tinted face cream and brushed her teeth, realizing she hadn't brought her clothes in the bathroom with her.

Not hearing anything, she decided to chance it and tiptoed across the hall in the towel, slipping into the office as quickly as she could, but not before she heard her laughter from the couch in the living room.

"Didn't know I was here, did ya, Rosie?" a muffled voice she knew well reached her through the wall.

Dammit, she'd been worried about Max when Matt had been there all along. Not that she cared about her brother seeing her in a towel that fully covered everything, but she wouldn't hear the end of it.

"Hey, we're going to go—" Max popped his head inside the room. Their eyes met as she gripped the towel together. He didn't look down, not that it didn't cover her, but that helped. "Sorry, Red. We're heading out to get some lunch. Want anything?" She swore she saw his eyes heat up at the last part, looking back at her. She swallowed past that damn frog in her throat again and shook her head.

"Okay, well if you get hungry, there's stuff in the kitchen. Make yourself at home. I'll be back after a while, don't let *anyone* in," he said, looking at her seriously. I mean, who did she know around here? It's not like she talked to many people, even in her own apartment unit.

The men left together, and Rose got dressed, pulling on her own loose pants and a lace tank top over a clean bra and panties. She layered a hoodie over it and pulled her wet curls into a loose pony with some heavy cream for the frizz. She pulled out her laptop, bringing it into the living room to work from the couch with her now cold coffee.

Despite it being Sunday, she pulled out her glasses and caught up on her emails a bit. She sent one to her lead researcher, letting him know she would be working from home this week after the excitement of last night's event, at least until they knew more.

Her phone pinged with a message.

Holy crap! I heard you almost died last night. (Kitty)

Well, kinda, but no. Lol (Rose)

I also heard you are staying with Max?! (Kitty)

Soooooo yeah. (Rose)

Why so tight lipped, I mean did you…? (Kitty)

NO. Omg. (Rose)

Well, there was a moment at the reception. I think. Idk. (Rose)

But def not sex. (Rose)

She wished. Well, she'd wished when she was 16. She'd so wanted him to be the one to take her virginity. Considering how awkward it had been a few years later with Brian, the guy she'd dated her first two years at college, and learning that most people's first times were weird, she wasn't too disappointed. More so embarrassed that she had begged him for that. I mean, not that it probably wouldn't be good now. Better than it had been with Brian, assuredly.

She flushed like someone could see her. But there was just Buck, watching her quietly from his bed with Luna. She needed to find the treat she had promised him.

I mean, if it happens, maybe don't fight it. It's been a long time comin. (Kitty)

Yeah, that's not happening. Lol (Rose)

Just maybe try to be open to possibilities? (Kitty)

Kitty knew her well. Rose tended to get into a rut with her expectations and often didn't see things coming her way. And then, when blindsided, she didn't always react logically, like when she had felt panicky in the kitchen earlier.

Getting over Max had taken a lot. Going back there just wasn't a good idea.

Chapter 4

Max

"**G**od, I am so glad you were there," Matt said roughly, rubbing his forehead and looking at Max after he had filled him in on the night before. Well, most of it. Not his overheated thoughts of his buddy's sister—before or after the chaos.

"I didn't realize how bad it was," Matt added, shocked. "She looks fine now."

Max still couldn't forget what Rose had looked like, crumpled against the bloody streaked wall, her dress torn, the rubble in her hair. He hadn't been able to breathe until he'd felt her pulse against his thumb and knew he'd had her.

He rubbed his scruffy chin. "Yeah, man, it was rough there for a minute."

The server brought them their plates, giggling as she set them down in front of them. She had definitely flirted a bit with them as she'd taken their orders, neither of them responding very much, other than politeness. But Matt gave her a gracious smile and thanked her.

"And my mom said you let her stay in one of your local apartments, man. I can't thank you enough," his friend thanked him for a second time since he'd gotten there. Max again reassured him that they were like family to him, and you always took care of family.

After Max had met Matthew that day in the schoolyard, they'd become fast friends. Both liked sports and girls already at that point. They quickly bonded over their family's shared Ranch lifestyle, although Max wasn't dumb. Even at that age, he knew they came from vastly different worlds. The Anderson name was old Texas money, although his mother had raised her sons to understand that this didn't mean they were any different from any other person, other than the privileges they were responsible for. Lisette Anderson hadn't grown up rich as their father had, and she taught her boys what she could of humility and the responsibility of the power they so naturally received.

So, when Max had gone over to the much smaller Montgomery Ranch to hang with his friend, Caroline Montgomery, Matt and Rose's mother, had felt much like his own. She'd taken him under her wing when he was there and looked after him, getting on to him when he'd done typical kid shit along with Matthew and hugging him whether he felt he needed it or not.

They'd usually gone to the Anderson house for the newest video games that were released, the two playfully competitive until they wound up on the same teams in high school. His forever wingman, the only time Matt hadn't known about a girl when he'd been around, was Red. And Max would never mention that, as he'd never do anything about it. Red had been like his kid sister until she wasn't. He remembered seeing her across the lunchroom, two years behind him, quietly reading her book as she ate her sandwich. He'd wished he were headed behind the bleachers with her, pissed at himself for the flash of unbidden desire for the younger girl. He'd long figured she hadn't thought a bit about him with her nose in her books. Until their eyes had met across that room of lunch tables that day and the rest of that school year after. That day in the truck between them had been building that whole year. He still didn't know how everyone else in their lives hadn't felt scorched by the looks between them like he had.

"I want you to be the one to fuck me, Max," she'd whispered in his ear as she had clenched her thighs around him in that truck bed. And it had startled him back to reality, just like the clatter of Matt's fork against his plate just did as he'd set it down.

"Well, I owe ya, man," Matt said before excitedly telling him about the newest bull he'd purchased while in town and his recent research and plans for the Montgomery Ranch as he'd begun to take over. Max knew Matt had been primarily running the Montgomery Ranch for years, but since their grandfather passed late last year, he'd finally become the sole decision-maker for the business. Matt had a good head on his shoulders and some good ideas to modernize the systems, as their grandfather had been old school and preferred it that way, resisting some of the changes over the decades that had kept them small.

Max himself had never been interested in following in his father's foot-steps in the ranching business. While he was on the board as part owner of Anderson Brother's Cattle, he'd been the least involved, really. Letting Nathan step up as the next leader in the family with their father had only felt natural. Nat lived and breathed cattle, so Max had never felt guilty when it came to Nat. But their father had been another story. When Max had taken a turn in interests his senior year of high school, actually quitting the football team to focus on the K-9 volunteer program he'd helped start with his Junior ROTC friends, he knew it had been a huge disappointment for his father. When they had started the program for the community service hours they'd needed for their honors classes, he'd never imagined how big it would become for the school or how invested he'd become in the JROTC.

With Max and Jackson focusing on other fields, their dad had eventually adjusted to the idea that maybe all three of his boys wouldn't be heavily invested in the company's day-to-day activities. Especially when they willingly participated in the annual board meetings and remained on call for unusual circumstances. But back then, he'd refused to fund Max's interest in the police academy. So, when the Lieutenant Colonel in his program talked with him about enlisting, the Marines eventually wound up being his way out.

Bringing his attention back to Matt, they finished up their meal. Matt paid this time, each usually taking turns when they caught up over drinks or food. Max heckled his friend as they walked out of the burger joint—the waitress had written her phone number on the receipt when she'd returned it, specifically handing it to Matt.

For the first time ever on the topic of women, Matt avoided eye contact as he expressed being too busy to date right now. Max thought about pushing for more info, but considering he was avoiding the topic of his best friend's sister, he thought he'd let it go for now. Matt would tell him if there was anything interesting happening in his life when he was ready.

They arrived back at his condo about an hour and a half after they'd left. Max figured Red would be dressed, trying to forget what wanting to peel the towel off of her felt like earlier. The previously scheduled lunch had been just what he needed to remind him that things needed to stay fully platonic between him and Red while she stayed with him. His only job was to protect her, and that included from himself if need be.

Matt stayed for another hour or so, sitting in the living room with the football game on until he needed to head out to a meeting to finish the paperwork on the cattle he'd acquired at the auction early that morning. Hugging his sister and telling her to stay away from explosives, he took off to finish business in time to return to Newheart for the evening chores. They had a few daytime hired hands on the Montgomery ranch, but Matt liked to be actively involved in the day-to-day work.

Max took Buck on a run around the complex while Red pulled a book out and got lost in it. He wasn't sure what to do about the awkwardness between them. If anything would help, it likely would be time. The last time he'd seen her before last night's event had been entirely too intimate for the just turned sixteen-year-old and the almost eighteen-year-old he had been. How does one come back from that and just be friends? Clearly, age wasn't a factor now. Both were accomplished in their own worlds, wiser for their years. But he just couldn't shake the feeling that he was responsible for shielding her innocence from him.

He'd known she dated over the years. Her brother had even mentioned some kid in college whom they'd thought she might marry young. He swallowed the old jealousy that threatened to rise, reminding himself that he hadn't been anything to her other than another big brother and a teenage crush.

He pretended to be interested in the end of the game rather than wondering what it would be like to move to the couch where she was, take her in his lap, and kiss the rise of her lace-edged breasts that peeked out at him through the slightly open zip of her sweatshirt.

He could only stand it so long before he knew his hardening state would be noticeable through his jeans, and he decided to take the dog out again. Buck looked at him strangely, as it was so soon after they had recently been out, but the wise older dog didn't mind, he loved the outdoors. They needed to get a hike in soon now that things were warming up with the spring sun.

He knew things would get easier tomorrow when they both had things to do with work and day-to-day living. She needed to rest today after the terror of last night and the recovery from her head wound. He'd been there when the doctor had reported that the head wound really did seem to be okay as long as there were no further complications with the concussion. Max had enough training to know what to watch for but had seen no signs of concern when he'd woken her the few times the night before.

Watching her sleep in his t-shirt, the pale ginger of her pussy peeking out at him when she'd flung away the bedcovers at first, had been a whole other concern as it had nearly undone him. It was all he could blame when her sassy ass had presented itself to him when she had turned over to go back to sleep, and he'd slapped it without thinking things through. But he'd just barely stopped himself from following up the unexpected graze of her softness by reaching between her thighs to stroke her and see if she was wet. It was most definitely not the night.

As if it ever would be.

She hadn't mentioned it today, and he had decided not to either. Maybe she hadn't remembered in her sleepy state. Thankfully, the second time he woke her had been easier, she'd allowed him to check her eyes quickly, and she had stayed under the covers. He'd decided to just let her sleep from there, knowing she'd likely be up in a few hours.

He'd thought the time on the elliptical would help him get his mind off her, but when he'd noticed her panicky eyes in the kitchen, he'd immediately wanted to protect her from whatever had made her feel that way. Just like he had a time or two when the too-aggressive fellow football players had hit on her, not yet aware that he and Matt would have their heads on a platter if they touched her, to be backed up by his brothers if need be.

She had always been a bit skittish. Matt had brought her to a few high school parties with him, but she had never really seemed to be happy at those. He'd usually find her in a quiet corner with whoever's home it was' pet, quietly talking to the fur ball rather than to other students. He'd always figured if Kitty had been allowed to come, she would have been okay. He had never been sure how that friendship had formed. Kitty would talk to anyone, no social anxiety there. But Kitty's Mom had always been a bit overprotective and didn't let her girls go out in the evenings. So, Rose had often been on her own. And his teenage self had dared not get too close in his often alcohol-induced state. Even then, he'd known better.

Running back up the steps with Buck, he hung the leash on the wall in the laundry room. The tiny meow of the kitten came around the corner, and he scooped her up as he entered the living area, and Buck went for his water bowl.

Red had fallen asleep on the couch, the sun just beginning to set and dimming the room in its faint light. He pulled the gray throw blanket off the corner of the couch and gently covered her. Tucking an errant curl behind her ear, he swore to himself that he would protect her from whatever it was that didn't sit well in his gut regarding that explosion the night before. She moaned a bit in her sleep and turned her cheek into his hand against the couch.

God, why did her skin have to be so soft? Even without makeup, she was so beautiful. She had always been so different from any of the other girls he had known over the years. Her ginger hair and pale skin tone, her freckles, her sea foam green eyes. While he'd always had a penchant for intelligent women, none had ever been as unique as she was or as quiet. He rather liked her kind of quiet, the challenge of drawing her out. He often thought some people talked too much and said too much of everything they were thinking. His brain rarely turned off either, but he generally didn't say what he was thinking, preferring to keep things close to his chest.

He decided to shower off the sweat from the short run, moving into his bedroom and stripping as he entered his bathroom. His bath had a separate walk-in shower and jacuzzi tub that had sold him on the place. The previous owner of this unit had had a thing for showers clearly, as this shower was larger than any he'd ever been in before, with tiny tan and black pebbled tiles smooth as sand trailing into the shower that curved back behind the frosted glass wall of the sink. A pebbled seat was at the far end of the long shower, with a shower head on each wall and a large rainfall shower overhead. It had taken him a little while to figure out the buttons on the control system at the entrance to the shower when he first moved in, but once he had, it had become one of his favorite places to be in the home.

After a brief shower, telling himself he didn't need to think about her and rub one out, that it would only make things worse, he put on a pair of sweatpants and a t-shirt. She was still sleeping, so he began to throw together a tossed salad for dinner and marinate two steaks to grill on the griddle on the commercial stovetop his mother had insisted he would need later.

He had to admit that an indoor grill was pretty awesome.

While he let her sleep a little longer, he turned on the lamp beside the easy chair and pulled out his laptop. He'd check on some of the updates from the lab on last night's explosion. He knew not everything would be completed with it being a Sunday. Not finding much, he reviewed a few pieces of evidence from other cases he'd recently turned in. He jotted down some notes next to a few items in the system and made a note for himself to follow up tomorrow.

As it circled past 8pm, he decided to check on her. It took a few attempts before she began to stir, throwing her arm over her eyes and grumbling at him to leave her alone, she was fine.

"Red," he chuckled, "Let me see your eyes," while trying to peel her arm off her face gently. Her eyes sleepily opened, her green eyes dark and glazed over as she looked at him intently.

"Stop waking me up if you're not going to do anything about it," she said grumpily, gently pushing at him, sitting on the edge of the couch. Her eyes opened a tad wider at herself after she said it, and he felt her anxiousness rise.

Her pupils were fine, but he couldn't look away from her. His hand came to rest on her cheek, smoothing the crease the blanket had made in her freckles. His thumb grazed her lower lip.

"You know none of that is a good idea," he said, contemplating his choices.

The tip of her tongue flicked his finger, and she gently bit it. No longer thinking, he pulled her up by her armpits and sat with her in his lap, his hands capturing the sides of her face as he took her mouth swiftly with his. She clawed at the sides of his shirt until he pulled it over his head, unzipping her sweatshirt in a swift movement and taking her breasts into his palms, filling them.

He ran his lips down the side of her neck, gently nipping there as he pulled her bra and tank top down, her nipples free to his thumbs. She moaned, leaning back she gave him easier access as he ran his lips down her freckled pale chest bone and gently nipped at her breast. She groaned and gripped his hair harder, so he increased the pressure and bit down more with his teeth on her nipple, his tongue grazing the rosy, pink bud.

God, this was moving so fast.

"Fuck, Red, we shouldn't..." he groaned, his cock hard against his thigh as she began to undulate her thighs against him.

Moving one leg over him to straddle him, she took him by the face and kissed him again, putting everything she could into the moment. She rubbed her pussy against him again, feeling his thick cock rubbing against her center despite the clothes in between them. Her curls had come loose from her hair band and were wantonly hanging down her back. He wanted to fist them so badly, but he thankfully remembered her head injury just in time and pressed his hands to her hips, stopping her movement against him.

She froze, but in a position that had him right against her clit, he knew. He could see the intensity of the arousal in her eyes. He had intended to stop things but instead found himself slipping his hand inside her sweatpants and panties, his thumb finding her wetness between them.

She began slowly moving again, her eyes rolling back into her head as she felt him circle her clit with her wetness. She squeezed her hips around him, much like she had oh so long ago. With one more circle of his thumb at her center, she came—her head rolling back as she breathed through the moment—her hair seemingly catching fire in the light from behind her. He gave her breasts one last appreciative stroke before he pulled her to him for a moment and then kissed her forehead regretfully.

"That can't happen again, Red," he said, his lips still on her forehead. He closed his eyes. *Dammit. That really couldn't.*

"Fuck, Max." She pulled back. Her eyes hurt. She had always been so expressive to him. "Is that what you say to all the girls you bring to an orgasm?" She pulled her shirt and bra back up and got up. He attempted to follow her, but she said, "NO. I need a minute." Then proceeded to shut herself in the bathroom.

Dammit. He'd known nothing good could come outta that. *Fuck him. Fuck his discipline.* He berated himself as he paced for a moment. Everything had all gone to shit so quickly.

He didn't know what to do, should he go to her, or maybe just start dinner? No, going to her was part of the problem in the first place. So, he decided to start dinner. He gritted his teeth as he heated the griddle. Why was this so fucked up? Why did they have to be attracted to each other? Why his best friend's kid sister?

He hung his head as his hands gripped the counter. He counted backward from 10 slowly, focusing on his breath.

He eventually placed the steak on the heated grill, bringing himself back into some semblance of control. The sound of the sizzle was somewhat satisfying as it seared the seasoned meat, and he focused on that. He got out the salad he'd premade and a few plates, along with a bottle of cabernet that would pair well with the meat. He had just set the steaks on the cutting board to rest when he heard her come back in.

She leaned against the fridge, arms crossed over her chest, looking at what he was preparing. She'd pulled her strawberry curls back up into a ponytail, and she was avoiding his eyes, but they were pink, and he could tell she'd been crying.

FUCK you, Anderson, his inner voice said again. And he deserved every bit of it.

She looked up to meet his eyes, and he caught the telltale tightening that dared him to talk about it.

"The silverware is in that drawer," he said, nodding his head to the one by the sink. "And the steak knives are in the block by the microwave." He got down two wine glasses and opened the cork with an automatic opener.

"I don't know that I've ever eaten at the table," he said, taking his plate and glass to the living room chair and giving her some space. It was better this way—even the awkwardness.

It was so much better than hurting her.

They ate in silence for a few minutes until he found a music channel to put on quietly. He searched for a safe topic for her, asking about her foundation and how it had started. She hesitantly began to speak, feeling more confident after a moment, with the topic clearly being a favorite for her. She filled him in on how she had begun to focus her senior year in high school on what she wanted to do, mentioning she'd been in therapy to help with social anxiety. Beginning to understand that her brain worked a little bit differently than others helped her understand how to navigate unusual social situations when she had to. Being intrigued by understanding the brain led down a road in science that only interested her more as she moved along in her degrees, eventually winding up with a Ph.D. in Neuroscience and Biology. But she didn't want to do any kind of practice directly with people, and she loved learning, as well as being a research assistant while in grad school. So, in seeking to do something that honored her father, who had died of a brain tumor when she was young, she had established the foundation with the money left to her from her Father's life insurance that had been kept in a trust for her until she turned 21.

He had known most of that, having heard it from Matt, but she didn't know that. And watching her eyes light up as she talked so intensely about something she was passionate about satisfied him in a way many things never did. He'd loved to hear her talking about whatever new interest she had taken on at any given time when they were younger, often around the sciences. She'd participated in STEM programs over the years, and her projects had been amazing, eventually even winning an award at the state level her senior year, he'd heard.

"Sorry," she said, "I've been talking too much. Sometimes things excite me." She glanced anxiously at him and then picked her fork and knife back up.

He just smiled. "Hearing about what you enjoy always pleases me." Then realized what he had said. *Well, shit.*

She glanced up, going still mid-bite. Their gazes locked. Fuck—the light of awareness in her gaze. How did she know about that shit? He flashed on their moment on the couch an hour or so ago. He shook his head at himself. She wasn't a child anymore. How she had sex and with whom wasn't his business.

He took another bite, methodically cutting his next three pieces of steak the exact same size and lining them up on the plate to busy his mind and give him a reason not to make further eye contact for a moment. He felt his protectiveness rise and tried not to think about her past relationships.

Rather than address his comment, he decided to shift the topic. He talked about leaving Newheart and entering the Marines. He skipped over the why, which seemed apparent in his mind, as he'd been way too old for her and was her brother's friend. There was no need to rehash that and it could lead to dangerous places. He talked about his father's disappointment and lack of support at first but how that had changed over the years as he still helped with ranch and family decisions at the board level and supported Nat anytime he could.

He brought up every subject he could, anything to avoid continuing the previous one. He eventually realized he was nervously chattering, which wasn't his usual thing.

Thankfully, Rose yawned. He latched on to the thought that it was late, and they both had to work in the morning. He mentioned he would probably go to the gym at work in the morning before getting his day started, so he'd be up and out at 0530. She was startled at the time he mentioned and said she'd see him later. She'd probably just work from there for most of the week. He told her he'd get a key made and walk her through the alarm system if she'd just hold tight for the day.

Lying in bed, all he could think about was how close she lay, not even a room away. He'd fucked things up pretty royally today. Somehow, he'd need to balance looking out for her and not being so close to her. Late into the night, he considered the impossibilities of that and how he could get her through this unscathed by the unknown terrors of the weekend—or himself.

Chapter 5

Rose

Rose lay on the surprisingly comfortable sofa bed late into the morning. She'd slept in a bit, but she'd lain there for at least an hour, wondering what the hell she was going to do about things.

Clearly, Max was attracted to her too. The more she thought about it, the more she realized the stuff at the charity event between them hadn't just been a blip, a figment of her imagination. Not after how hot things had been between them yesterday on his couch. And his comment, the slip about being pleased? And then avoiding addressing it. She was too intelligent not to follow the arrows. So many things added up. Max had always tended to be protective of others.

She knew he looked at her as just being Matt's little sister quite often. Hell, they all had seemed to decide for her that he needed to take care of her with this damn bomb thing. It was like everyone thought Max should take care of Rose, and no one even asked her about it.

But she'd explored some stuff in the last relationship she had had that her family hadn't known about because she hadn't brought Kevin home. The truth was, she'd pretty much never seen the relationship going beyond the sexual exploration that it was. But exploring BDSM with Kevin had actually been helpful for her social anxiety. They had parted ways amicably, as Kevin was poly, and Rose just wasn't sure she saw herself staying that route. Also, Max had truly never left her head. She had just accepted that he wasn't for her, no matter how much she had cared in the past.

There was no way 'pleasing him' wasn't a reference to BDSM...

Rose lay there for a bit and allowed her mind to wander, imagining a Dominant Max. It fit. Like a glove, really. And turned her the hell on. For a moment, she allowed her fingers to travel down her body, stopping to play with her nipples for a moment as she thought about his beard, lips, and teeth on them the day before. One hand slipped further down into her pajama shorts sans panties. She imagined his thumb on her clit, the way he had felt against her beneath his pants. Imagined him commanding her the way he must have his team in the Marines... only... different.

Her clit throbbed. It ached so much for more of what hadn't been finished between them yesterday.

She got up, frustrated. She hadn't brought anything with her, like a vibrator. She used to rub against a pillow when she was younger, imagining it was Max. But she knew it wouldn't be enough. She took a shower instead, which really didn't help much, as she ran her slippery hands over her body with soap and the sponge. Thoughts of Max stepping into the shower from behind her and his hands following hers kept slipping into her mind, but it just left her more and more frustrated.

How was she supposed to go back to the way things were? Knowing he wanted her too but felt he somehow had to protect her from him or stop something from happening because she was Matt's kid sister? She was a goddamned adult and could fuck whomever she wanted, damn it.

Only the thought of saying that *scared the shit out of her.*

She wrapped herself in a towel and headed back to the office. Leaving the door open since no one was home, Luna came and found her as she was zipping her jeans. She had a class to teach at 11, so she added a cardigan over the lacy tank and her Montgomery Ranch logo necklace her mother had designed a few years back. She twisted her hair on top of her head into a curly top knot and added a light touch of foundation and mascara for the camera. She filled a coffee cup and settled at the desk to prepare for her class.

After her Introduction to Neuroscience class, she logged into the laboratory systems and reviewed recent reports for the research project she collected data for at the local University clinic. She tracked and evaluated for a while until she decided to take a break around two and find something to eat. She played with Luna for a bit, then put together a sandwich and some veggie slices. She eventually returned to work for a few more hours on the book she had been slowly putting together to be published by the University.

She decided to stop around 6 pm when her Momma called to check on her. She hadn't heard from Max all day, but she hadn't really expected to. She had texted a little bit with Kitty during her lunch break.

She wasn't sure what Max had planned to do for dinner. She blanked for a little while on what to do. She didn't want to assume they would have dinner together. He might have other plans. When 8 o'clock came and went, she decided to make herself a small salad with what was left of the veggies. She and Luna snuggled on the couch for a while, watching television, but Max and Buck still weren't home when she decided to eventually head to bed. She had an early class tomorrow at 8 am, and she did not enjoy getting up early.

She left a note on the counter for Max.

Max~
It would be helpful to know what to expect in the evenings. Also, how to not be a prisoner in the condo, as lovely as it is. We need a grocery plan. I have a virtual class at 8am.
Rose

Getting ready for bed, Rose heard the house phone ring in the kitchen. Not thinking much of it, she ignored it, as it wasn't her home. But as she lay there in the dark, it kept ringing. Finally, after multiple rounds of calls, she got up and headed to the kitchen, where the cordless phone was on the wall. The caller started another round of calls.

"Hello?" Rose answered. Silence.

"Hello?" Rose said again, waiting. She thought she heard breathing on the other end, not heavy or unusual, just a soft breath.

Click. The person had hung up their end of the call.

Strange, but the calls seemed to have finally stopped. So, Rose headed back to bed. She hadn't intended to, but she must have slept lightly until Max got home. Rolling over, she glanced at her watch and saw 11:35 pm after she heard the garage open and close. She heard him and Buck enter quietly, shuffling around in the living room and kitchen. She heard him pause and read the note she'd left, wondering what he had thought about all day. Surely not like she had thought about him in bed and the shower earlier today since she hadn't heard anything from him, despite his now having her number after she put it in his phone the other night. She felt him pause by the office door, which she'd closed since she had Luna with her, but then move on to his bedroom.

She turned over, pulling the pillow over her head, wishing she could turn off her brain and stop the ruminating. Sheep were useless.

He started the coffee at 5:30 the next morning and grabbed his shoes to take Buck for a quick run. Although he didn't have to go in today until noon, he liked keeping his sleep routine as consistent as possible. The morning was cool, so he grabbed a zipped sweatshirt before grabbing the leash and heading out.

He knew he'd left her hanging all day yesterday. He'd started a text about five different times but deleted it each and every time. Each one sounded like he was apologizing, or sounded like a relationship check-in. He also hadn't thought it would be as late as it had been, but he'd decided on dinner with a few friends after work to avoid the intimacy of the night before. It had been an easy out, a coward's way out. He should have at least texted her. He knew that.

He was considering calling the number of the waitress at their usual bar to see if she wanted to grab a drink.

Did he want to? No, not really. He had a lot on his plate with work, and now he had the bomb situation at the charity event added to it, and now navigating things with Rose. But he needed to. Maybe set some expectations for himself regarding the limits of his connection to Rose. Maybe get out a little sexual frustration if things went the way he thought they might, based on the fingertip Leslie had grazed down his thigh when she thought no one was looking last night. They'd flirted a little before when Max had gone there after work, it was a bar for cops. She had a bit of a reputation for cop-hopping, and he knew he wasn't the only cop she flirted with. Plus, it had never really moved beyond flirtation, and Max didn't tend to push what didn't feel right.

But every time he thought about texting Leslie, he'd flash on the image of a bloody and unconscious Rose lying crumpled against the stage wall, and his stomach would turn.

He owed Red an apology and needed to figure out how to make this work for the short term.

His phone rang in his ear.

"Anderson," he answered curtly.

"Hey, bro," said Jackson. "How ya holding up?" His younger brother had always been an earlier riser like he was. Gotta get shit done.

"Fine," Max responded curtly, unsure why Jackson would be asking that. "Why, what's up?"

"Well, I know Rose is staying with you..." Jackson trailed off.

"Yeah," Max said, "Nothing new from the labs though yet that I know of."

"Well, I mean, it's Rose," said Jackson. Max waited for him to elaborate.

"I mean, you..." Jackson said hesitantly, "Rose is, or at least was, somehow always importantly awkward for you."

What? He'd never said a word to anyone about that night happening. *Anyone.* "What the hell are you talking about? Come on Jax. It's not like you to not get to the point," Max said bluntly.

"Okay, don't get pissed at me. But I know you avoid talking about Rose when her name comes up. You always looked out for her, and she always looked up to you with those puppy dog eyes of hers. And then there was suddenly nothing. I don't know how, and I don't know when, but you and Rosebud had some kind of run-in, and you aren't telling anyone, which only says that something happened somewhere along the way," Jackson said plainly. "You can deny it, but bro, I always figure stuff out. You know I do."

Shit. Max methodically counted his foot strikes on the cement to ten before responding. "There is nothing between Rose and me," he said honestly. Well, partially honest, since there couldn't be, even after the other night. "I'm not, and never have been, seeing Red." Maybe saying it out loud would make it feel more real.

"Yeah. M'kay, big bro. Keep avoiding it, if that's what you want to tell yourself," Jackson told him. "I saw how you moved to protect her. Not just even when she was hurt in the explosion but after. You didn't offer for Uncle Andy to stay at your place."

"She'd like a fucking sister to me, Jax! She's Matt's sister," Max exploded for a moment, before he caught his breath again. He refused to lie but he was not admitting anything to his youngest sibling either. "And fuck, you should see the shitty security she had in her place, bro. We hooked Uncle Andy's up, he's good."

"Uh-huh," Jackson said. "All true, I'm sure. I know you, though, bro. I see your response to her. And I know your protective streak. But Max, life isn't always going to work out with the cookie-cutter rules you expect it to. Sometimes life gets a little messy... And sometimes it's better that way." Jackson had softened his tone.

Max remained silent. He knew that. But he didn't want to hurt Rose, of all people. He was willing to let his life get messy, if need be, but he would fucking protect her from it.

He ran in place for a moment before entering his unit. "I gotta go, Jax. Love you, bro," and he signed off—thinking about what his brother said but not being willing to flex on this one. Plus, he didn't mess with his brother's on-again, off-again unconventional relationships and chaos. *Why did Jax need to mess with his?*

After getting inside, he hung up the leash, handing Buck a treat and feeding him his breakfast. He dried off his face with his hoodie and threw it directly into the washer, wet with sweat. His shorts were too, but Rose was here. Turning the corner out of the laundry room, he saw that she stood at the counter sleepily yawning, pouring a cup of coffee. He hadn't expected her to be up yet. Even with her 0800 class, 0600 was early, and he knew she preferred to sleep in.

Turning to face him, she leaned against the counter, her little white sleep tank and shorts an imagination minefield as she definitely didn't have on a bra and possibly even panties as the short's camel-toed a bit. He groaned internally.

"Good morning," he said carefully, uncertain of her mood—both from the earliness of the morning and from her note last night. He grabbed a coffee cup and filled it, taking a breath before looking back at her. He leaned against the island, shirtless in his running shorts, as he looked across at her. He carefully focused on her eyes—which didn't look happy.

"It's 6am, Max. Most people in the world aren't having a good morning yet," she grumbled, sipping the coffee, and closed her eyes for a moment as she struggled to wake up. She'd always hated waking up early, he remembered, chancing a glance down her body again, noting her tightened nipples, and when his eyes rose back to hers, he knew she had seen.

She raised an eyebrow. "I need food plans, and probably a grocery run. And this 'don't ever leave the condo' thing is really for the birds. I need out now and then." She rolled her eyes. "Even pets get fed and walked."

She was right. He gestured to her note, where he'd already laid the extra key and written the passcode to the alarm with a few brief instructions. He'd written it all out last night when he wasn't sure they'd see each other this morning.

"There's the key, Red," he said, softening his tone, "and the alarm instructions. I'm sorry I left you hanging yesterday. It wasn't intended. I hadn't expected to be out so late." Which felt close to a lie, but he really hadn't planned it. He had just avoided getting up to come home as the minutes ticked by, and he hadn't actually texted her, despite overthinking it.

"Listen," she said, her voice getting frustrated. "This whole thing wasn't my idea. I'm happy to stay at my place. You can let me know when you hear something." She glanced at the phone. "Oh yeah, there was a weird hang-up call last night."

His coffee sloshed in his cup as his eyes flicked abruptly to meet hers. "What do you mean?" he asked sharply.

"I don't know," she said flippantly, "Guess you shoulda been here." She began to move past him. He grasped her arm, turning her towards him as she passed.

"Tell me what happened, Rose," he said firmly.

She rolled her eyes. "I'm sure it wasn't a big deal. As I said, maybe you should have been here." She tried to pull her arm out of his hand and turn away.

"Red," he said, his voice low and stern.

"What?" she said, voice raising a bit and frowning. "Why do you call me that anyways? I'm not some kid who follows you around like a puppy dog anymore, dammit."

"Fuck," he said, losing his temper a little. "Don't you know that I know that? Can't you tell that I do everything in my power not to react to the fact that you grew up long ago, and I couldn't avoid that?" He cupped her chin firmly. "Rose, you goddamn set me on fire when you look at me like that, and *that* is why I've always called you Red."

He took her face in his hands, and then he kissed her, pressing her against the refrigerator. She nearly climbed him, wrapping her legs around him, and he lifted her ass into his hands, pressing his already rock-hard cock into her soft, barely covered pussy.

She mewled and ran her fingers through his curls, clenching and pulling his face closer to hers. He felt her pebbled nipples through her tank rubbing against his naked chest.

"God dammit, Red," he said, his mouth still against hers, his tongue snaking out to lace with hers for another heated moment. He paused, pressing his forehead against hers. "We can't do this." He closed his eyes, searching for self-control.

"Why not?" she said softly. "I won't break, Max. I'm not a china doll, and I sure as hell am not sixteen anymore."

He groaned and opened his eyes. He looked deep into her green ones that had darkened to a shade of evergreen with passion. He slid his thumb across her pebbled breast over the thin tank. "I know you aren't a kid. Do you think this feels like I think you're a kid, Red?" Her breath hitched faster as he plucked the tight little nub with his fingertips.

He slipped his hand lower inside her shorts—goddamn it, no panties like he'd thought—and slid easily between her folds and caressed her already wet clit. She closed her eyes and tipped her head back against the refrigerator. "Does this feel like I think you are a goddamned child, Red?"

He leaned into her, holding her up against the refrigerator as he pressed his raging hard cock between her hips, grinding against her heat. "Does this feel like I think you are just my friend's kid sister, Red?" he whispered gutturally into her ear as he bit the tip of it and flicked her nipple again with his other hand.

She groaned, but she slipped a hand between them and slid it into his shorts and took ahold of his length. She looked pleadingly at him. "Please, Max?"

It was the same goddamned thing she had said to him so many years ago, with those same fuck me, mermaid siren eyes. Back then, it had scared the shit out of him, hearing her say the words he knew fit so well into the kinky shit he had just started to try out as a kid of almost 18. Dominance had given him a sense of control of his world, a sense of responsibility for another, which fit his nature so well. But hearing her beg him—that same needy 'please,' when she had always been so innocent to him—had sent him down an emotional landslide as a teenager.

But today, she was right. She was an adult and clearly had some sort of experience with this. He took her by the chin and drew her down to kneel in front of him. Looking up at him with those big seafoam-green eyes, she slid his shorts and boxer briefs down over his ass as she took him into her hand. Looking down at him, she worshiped him with her eyes and then her mouth, taking him softly between her lips.

The feel of her silky mouth made his knees weak, and he held himself up by leaning on the fridge over her. When she took him deep into her throat, he nearly lost it. *How had she grown up so goddamned much, and who did he have to kill that taught her how to do goddamn that.* He reached down, and careful of her still healing head wound, he held the side of her cheek and neck as he began to fuck her mouth. GOD DAMN *FUCK.*

"Goddamn it, Red," he said throatily, pulling her back up and pushing her towards the couch. She wiggled down her shorts as she walked in front of him, and he smacked her ass without thinking twice, checking off a boyhood fantasy. She jumped and turned, laughing, and he pushed her back against the back of the couch, kissing her again and pulling her tank down beneath her breasts. She leaned over the back of the couch a bit as he nipped her breast, but then he turned her around, bending her forward and sliding his hand down between her legs from behind and felt her soaking little pussy.

"God, please, Max..." she panted, nearly climbing the couch as she arched her ass towards him.

"Fuck... Rose, I need my wallet," he said, needing a condom, and started to back up. Plus, they didn't need to do this here, the first time between them, when a bed wasn't that far away.

"I'm good," she said over her shoulder. "I recently tested negative and IUD—I promise. Just please..." she begged, arching her back as she reached down and slipped her hand between her legs, grinding against her own palm and rubbing her clit.

"Impatient, are you?" He slid his hand under her right knee and brought it up on the back of the couch as he slipped his fingers inside her wetness from behind. He lined his cock up with her sweet little hole and rubbed against her wetness, making sure she was ready for him. When she mewled again and flicked her clit, the tip of her finger grazed his cock, and he moaned and slid home.

Cause God, it felt like home.

"Fuuuuuuuck, Red," he said, groaning as he fit so perfectly. She arched her ass more as she began to flick faster at her clit. He gripped her waist and arched into her from behind, his hand sliding around to anchor himself by her breasts, catching her nipples between his fingertips. Arching his cock into her again and again, he felt her already beginning to come and spasm on his cock, clenching around him as he went quickly over the edge behind her.

"Maxxxxx..." she breathed, as she leaned into the couch, her back arching as she mewled into the orgasm. He pumped into her a few last times and groaned as he felt the last of his orgasm connect with hers. Fuck, how did they not even make it to the bed? They both panted for a moment, leaning over her against the couch, soothing her nipples with what energy he could find.

After a few breaths, he finally picked her up and brought her with him to sit on the couch. He was fully naked. She was just in her little tank top, still pulled below her breasts. He suspected she was somewhat embarrassed as she tucked her head beneath his against his chest, that or tired—or both.

He gave them another minute to catch their breath. He hadn't seen that coming, and he needed to recalculate. Eventually, when the sun was streaming in the windows, he tucked his finger under her chin and tipped her chin up so he could meet her eyes.

Yep, there was that embarrassment.

"Welllll," he drawled. "No room for feeling embarrassed now, Red. This little fire of ours has crawled up my ass, and now we've both been a little singed." He smiled, winking, trying to lighten the moment between them. She cracked a small, faint smile, but her cheeks turned pink, again reinforcing his suspicions. "This isn't done. But have you noticed the time?"

She shook her head, eyes widening, mentioning she didn't have on her watch. When he told her it was 0730, she scrambled up and off him and the couch and raced for the bathroom. "I—I promise I will be back—or we'll talk about this—or whatever. But I have class and need to shower."

He let her go, knowing she needed to prepare. "I was going to run to the grocery store while you had class," he called out. "I don't need to head into work today until noon."

He heard her turn on the shower through the door. "Okay, how about some turkey meat and whole wheat bread for sandwiches? More salad stuff would be good too. I'd like some fruit, and then veggies and meat of some kind for dinners would work too. Thanks, Max!" she yelled back, already in the shower.

He pulled his shorts back on for now. He'd shower after the grocery store and not disturb her hot water. He pulled a new shirt on and grabbed his keys, telling Buck to stay and be good. He laughed and told Luna the same, as she went racing past him with the morning zoomies.

While selecting various items at the store, he tried to keep himself from the existential dread that loomed. Really his brother was right, as was Rose. She was an adult, as was he. Their families didn't really need to know they were exploring whatever this was between them until they wanted them to, especially Matt. Maybe they just needed to burn this old fire out. If he was going to be keeping an eye out for her, there was no better time, really, since they'd be so close.

This could work out without tearing everyone apart, right? Including Rose?

Chapter 6

Rose

Rose finished the class with her brain halfway online.

Holy shit. She and Max had fucked. Like really fucked. Like not just a little, but over the goddamn back of the couch, bent over and fucking her fucked. Rose wasn't sure what to do with that. She would have never imagined that going down the way it did, but dear god, it was even better than she had imagined the morning before. She was half nervous that he was going to pull back and get all protective again when she went back out there.

She could hear him shuffling around in the kitchen, having gotten back from the store a few minutes before her class ended.

What does one say to the crush of your life after fucking over ten years later? Sometimes she couldn't pull words out of her mouth if someone paid her. She was horribly afraid this might be one of those times, no matter how often Max had always been one of the few who could draw her out.

But she wasn't going to get this awkwardness over by hiding in the office.

She opened the door and stepped back into the hallway, slowly making her way to the kitchen, where she could hear him moving around. Luna zipped past her as she entered the open space from the hallway, and she laughed as the kitten almost tripped her.

"She is so friggin cute when she does that," Max said, reaching immediately for her hand and pulling her close to him as he leaned against the counter. He tipped up her chin when she dropped her eyes. "No, don't do that. There isn't any reason to be embarrassed about this." He traced her lower lip as she met his eyes, the tip of her tongue automatically sneaking out to follow the trail he made and flicked the tip of his finger.

His eyes darkened. "This has been a long time coming between us, Red." He cupped her chin and drew her in for a soft kiss. Lost quickly in his lips, she felt him pull back and rest his forehead against hers again. Oh god, please don't let him stop all this now.

"We need to talk about some of this, though," he said, "Make sure we're on the same page." Taking her by the hand, he pulled her again to the couch, turning off the tv as he sat and pulled her into his lap. Kissing her forehead, she pulled back quickly, afraid he was going all big brother on her. She turned quickly, swinging a leg over his lap, and faced him.

"Listen," she said quietly, knowing it was now or never. "We don't have to make this more than it is." She wiggled on his lap to prove a point, knowing she felt his cock hardening beneath her.

"You can't tell me you don't feel this between us," she said, working up her courage. "I know you noticed it at the event the other night too. So, if we are going to be spending the next few days, weeks, or whatever this close together while we figure out what the hell is going on with that bomb situation, we might as well at least have some fun."

She saw the laughter in his eyes and pushed a little further. She wasn't just a kid to be humored. She leaned forward and went with her gut, capturing his lower lip between her teeth gently as she nipped. His eyes darkened again. His hand came to tangle gently in the side of her hair, opposite from her wound, as her lips trailed down his neck. "We don't need to tell any of our families about all of this, as I'm sure whatever it is won't even last, and we'll go our separate ways eventually."

She felt him stiffen slightly, and she pulled back. Her eyes met his, noticing his gaze had hardened as if a wall had come up between them. She wasn't sure what she had said wrong there, but he seemed to have decided something when he moved to slide his hands down her arms and pulled them together behind her back.

"It sounds like you have everything all figured out already, Red." He held her wrists firmly with one hand, the other trailing down the neck of her blouse. He flicked the top button open to reveal the edge of the lace at the top of her bra.

"I... I... I thought about it a little bit yesterday," she said, her breath catching at the dark look in his eyes as they followed his finger over the rise of her breasts peeking through.

"I see," he said, his voice dropping low. "Since you have all the details worked out, why don't you tell me what you thought about?" he asked, flicking open another button.

"I—well... I wouldn't say I have all the details worked out exactly," she hesitated, breathing heavily. *She was so not telling him about her thoughts from the other morning... or about touching herself.*

He tightened his hold a bit, pulling her arms further back, raising her chest towards him. The blouse fell open, a 3rd button now gaping the silky softness nearly to her belly button. She knew her pale green lace bra didn't really cover much, it wasn't padded, and the lace was see-through—her nipples catching against the lace as they strained for his attention.

"Tell me, Red," he said, his tone firmer as he looked at her intently. "Don't leave anything out."

His commanding tone heightened her senses. She didn't even notice her usual nerves as she began to tell him. "Well, I woke up thinking about us the night before. Ya know, on the couch." He trailed his forefinger down her neck and along the lace of the bra, teasing closer and closer to her pebbled nipples through the lace.

"And?" he asked quietly.

"Well, I touched myself," she said, blushing.

"Where did you touch yourself, Red?" he asked, his eyes rising to hers and holding.

"My... my breasts," Rose whispered. "A-a-and my clit." She could barely breathe as his eyes held hers. He grazed her nipple through the bra not once, not twice, but three times slowly as he held eye contact with her.

"Here?" he asked, waiting til she nodded. His hand slid lower and undid the snap of her jeans. Never breaking eye contact, he slipped his hand inside her panties.

"And here?"

Her breath hitched. His fingertip slowly circled the already throbbing and wet little nub. She lost focus, rolling her eyes back as she lulled her head back, curls cascading down her back. He stilled.

"Red? Was it here? You never answered..." He flicked again but then stopped and waited for her response.

"Yes, yes, fuck yes," she got out, simply wanting him to continue. Her ass instinctively ground against his cock nestled beneath her as she tilted her hips to him for access.

He jerked her arms tighter, bringing her breasts close as he used his teeth to draw her bra below a nipple, taking the nipple in his mouth and suckling before beading the nipple between his teeth as he increased the speed of his fingertip at her clit.

"And did you come, Red? Thinking about me?" he ground out against her skin.

"No, dammit," she blurted. "It was so fucking frustrating!" But her hips kept rocking against him, increasing the friction of his hand against her.

"And do you want to come now, Red?" he asked her, his voice dropping low as he slipped two fingers inside her, circling her clit even faster with his thumb.

She felt how hard his cock was beneath her as she clenched her ass against him and blurted out that she would rather come with his cock inside her instead. She hadn't been sure he would do it, but he took her by the waist and stood her in front of him and quickly divested her of her jeans and panties, and she climbed right back on him, with his shorts pulled down just enough that his cock slid right into her as she knelt on both sides of his legs. Rising up, he undid the last of her shirt buttons, pulling both breasts above her bra now as he filled his palms with her. She slid down on him again, noticing how fucking well he fit inside her.

"Fuuuuuuck…" she groaned. She didn't have anything against a good swear word or two, yet this was getting excessive. But fuuuuuuck he felt so good. Sex had never been this good for her. I mean, it was fine, but with Max…

When he was touching her, it was like all anxiety was gone, and all that ran through her was goodness and light. And just a little bit of dark sexy. She dropped her head back and felt his hand trace her neck, running down her chest and back up again. She rose and lowered herself, remembering all the times she had humped her pillow at night, thinking about Max Anderson between her legs. Fuck, that had nothing on this. He pulled her arms behind her again, capturing them with one hand as he used the other to slide between the two of them and circle her clit, almost immediately pushing her over the edge as he pressed down on her hip and pounded up into her.

"Fuuuuuuck. Red…" he grated out as he slipped over the edge himself, his head rearing back as his hips came up off the couch.

She collapsed onto him afterward, and they lay there breathing deeply. His hands rose to lazily slide up and down her arms, soothing the over-stimulation. Eventually, she leaned back up. She slipped her breasts back into her bra, but they were still connected as his cock slowly receded. He held her hips there with one hand. His other brought her chin up for eye contact.

"I want to see what's here between us, Red," he said softly. "But I think there is wisdom in not talking about it with our families, for now at least." His hand caressed her naked hip.

"Okay," Rose responded. I mean, it had been her idea. She didn't want to mess with his and Matt's friendship any more than he did. Especially if things didn't go anywhere. She would be damned cautious with her heart, though. There was way too much history for her when it came to emotions with him. Sex, she could focus on. Sex, no matter how passionate, could still be logical. Even the kinky shit. At least in her experience.

She pulled back and stood up, needing to go clean up. "Speaking of the family, though," she mentioned as she moved towards the bathroom. "Mine will expect me for family dinners on Fridays. You know they would always welcome you. Or I could take my own car and go."

She heard him sit there for a moment or two more before he got up. "No. You're not going alone," he said firmly as he passed the bathroom and headed into his room. "I need a shower. And I need to know more about the phone call yesterday, by the way. I didn't forget."

She cleaned herself up, sliding back into her panties and jeans and zipping them back up with the lacy blouse. Her hair had been fully down before, tamed and all, but sweat and sex had changed that, so she pulled it on top of her head and twisted it in a top knot with a few pins. *Definitely worth it.*

Feeling a tad bit more presentable despite not having any further classes today, she took her laptop and a book into the living room and curled up in what was beginning to feel like her corner of the couch. She found she enjoyed this spot. Luna often cuddled up in the crook of her knees or down with Buck when he was home, like now.

Max came back out from his shower, loose curls wet and slicked back for the moment, still having not shaved, she noticed appreciatively. His collar length, messy dark waves, and the thick, bearded aftergrowth were sexy as hell and only reminded her they weren't kids anymore. *She still remembered how delicious that beard felt against her skin.*

He was tying a blue tie, the crispness of his likely tailored dress shirt gleaming against his tan skin as he mentioned he would be out late tonight. They had a stakeout planned, and he and Buck were needed to assess for explosives in the facility. She mentioned that she likely wasn't going anywhere, just that it was nice to have the option and food.

She told him she really didn't know much more about the unusual call she had mentioned the night before other than they had kept calling quite a few times before she finally answered. He mentioned that it was strange, mainly because it was an unlisted number, he really only used it as a backup line in an emergency, but he'd look into a few things. He also showed her how to turn off the ringer if needed again, mentioning he would text or call her cell if he needed her.

"Uh-huh, like you had yesterday?" she teased him.

"Dammit, Red! I'm sorry!" he laughingly insisted, as he walked by her with Buck's food for the evening and placed it in his bag. Buck had noticed the preparations to leave and had stationed himself by the door, waiting. Luna circled him curiously, seemingly wondering where he was going.

Max stopped by where she was sitting and tucked a curl behind her ear.

"If it helps to know, I was really just trying not to think about you because thinking about you was all the fuck I was doing," he said honestly, his gaze intent on her. She swallowed, trying not to feel the feelings she was feeling.

"I'll likely see you in the morning," he said, brushing a soft kiss on her forehead as he and Buck headed out. She wasn't sure how she felt about those forehead kisses. While they felt warm and safe and made her soul happy, her head wasn't so sure they weren't based on his still thinking of her as a child. Time would tell. As would her emotions.

But she wasn't listening to that side of her brain today.

Max

Max felt okay about where things were between him and Rose if he didn't listen too closely to the quiet voice within asking him if all this was wise.

Instead, after he got a few things prepared for tonight's work, he focused on tracing the hang-up call that Red had told him about. Digging a little deeper, he found the number had come from a medical research lab that funded a pharmaceutical giant. Interesting. He texted his uncle and checked to see if he could stop by that afternoon for a brief chat. He didn't like to discuss evidence over the phone.

He'd briefly input his contact info into Rose's cell this morning after he'd realized she couldn't have even contacted him if she'd wanted to yesterday. *He had been such an idiot.* He quickly shot her a text.

See, I texted. (Max)

Uh huh (Red)

Glad you know how to use your phone. (Red)

Yeah, he'd show her what he knew how to use. Smart ass that she was, she'd always brought a smile to his face with her sass when she was younger. Something about the 'fuck you' attitude when you least expected it out of her quiet little mouth had always sparked his energy. He thought about a few things he was free to do with that mouth over the next few weeks and shifted uncomfortably in his jeans.

Down boy, he commanded himself. Self-control was his thing, but he was reminded that he had held back for a long, long time regarding her when everything he'd ever fantasized about came rushing back at him at once. Hiking. Shower sex. In the car. While riding a horse together. In his childhood bedroom. Taking her to one of the BDSM clubs in the area.

Buck raised his head and yipped once at him, sensing his tension. Max motioned him to rest easy with his hand, and he took a breath to settle himself.

He checked the lab reports on a few things, including the explosion from the weekend. A few new facts appeared in the report that he noted to follow up on later. One, in particular, he began to trace to verify. Cross-checking a few systems, he found himself at multiple dead ends, so he sent a secure message to Kris, an old school friend from Newheart in the local Dallas Bureau's Cyber Division and asked for assistance when she could. She had access to more loopholes and illegal backdoors than he did.

He really needed to grab coffee with her soon and catch up. He hadn't seen her since the last event they both worked at The Saddle Club here in Dallas. Max had just moved back to the States when an old friend who owned the ritzy kink club had asked him to step in and oversee an event while he was out of town. Kris had been working double as security and lead Domme supervisor. Max had recognized her from high school but hadn't thought too much about knowing her until he ran into her again at the FBI offices the next week. He should have made the connection after her security work. She was good at what she did—both security and Domme work. They had never really talked about how to manage knowing each other from both worlds, kink and professionally, but seemed to have silently agreed not to discuss their rare part-time gig at The Saddle Club at their primary employment on the rare occasion they were both working a case.

Max didn't work kink events very often. They just didn't line up with his schedule very well. He didn't really need the money, doing it more as a favor for his friend. But he could imagine the lucrative event nights balanced out the somewhat meager county salary for her.

He wrapped up the paperwork for a case he'd finished the week before, reviewing everything to make sure all the i's and t's had been dotted and crossed, wanting nothing missing when the case went to the state prosecutor's office. He knew he was likely to get called to testify on that one, and the less they had to tear apart, the more straightforward the questioning would be.

He fed Buck for the evening and grabbed a sandwich from the cold vending machine in the small cafeteria the city had put in a few years ago. The bread was a bit soggy, but he didn't mind too much as he needed the energy to focus tonight. He took Buck out for a brief walk to burn some late afternoon energy as the sun began to set, and he began to prepare his mind for the night.

He'd trained for the internal investigation unit in the Marines later into his military career, having decided to retire Buck after their active duty in the field with the Explosive Ordnance Disposal unit had come to an end. But as Staff Sergeant, Max had felt responsible for setting an example of integrating into civilian work. Their unit had sought to recover from the loss of his eldest tech, Sergeant Matthews, who had been caught by a landmine they had been unaware of while on their final assignment. Max decided to stay stateside after his unit returned. He had wanted to be closer to his family, so he eventually turned down the teaching position offered to him in the Marine Corps Criminal Investigations Division at Quantico and accepted the new position in the Dallas Police Department instead. The position was initially open for general detective work. When he'd applied for it with his background in explosives, though, the Chief had offered him the position to expand the department's local tools. So, when Buck didn't take well to retirement and being left home alone all day, the Chief had quickly come on board with Max's request to bring the trained Shepherd to work with him.

Dallas had a decent Canine Squad that had been around for decades with multiple branches and the insurance to support it. Max checked in with the program's Sergeant periodically, as on paper, Buck was a part of the larger district-wide unit. Max preferred to be more of a loner in his work, however, and had been given leeway to work on his own within reason as the only on-campus K-9 at their precinct location. He knew not everyone understood the shift in his career, but Max had never been driven by success, and the corruption he felt within the power of leadership gave him a bad taste in his mouth. Not that policing was much better. But he respected his Chief's hard line for dirty cops and liked that this position often allowed him to work alone.

He loaded Buck into the Explorer after they had circled back around to the station. He couldn't help but wonder what Luna and Red were doing, likely curled up on the couch or in bed, as it was late. Almost as if she had thought about him at the same moment, his phone pinged with a text.

> *I think you mentioned you leave early on Wednesdays, right? (Red)*

> *I don't plan to get up early. My class isn't until 11. (Red)*

> *Yes. Hadn't thought that far ahead. I should be home by 5pm or so tho tom. (Max)*

> *Okay (Red)*

> *Think of me tonight, when your hands are in your panties? (Max)*

What panties? I don't sleep with them. It's healthier that way. (Red)

Shit. Healthier for his cock. Even her overly logical nature sometimes got in his pants. He didn't respond as he drove to the position he had been assigned about a block from the targeted warehouse. He had an hour or so to wait, reporting anything unusual he observed. Buck sat next to him patiently in the front seat, his ears cocked and alert, knowing they were working.

> *You don't ever sleep with them huh? (Max)*

Rarely. It's good to air things out. (Red)

He smiled, knowing she still wasn't following his thoughts quite yet.

> *Are you in your pajamas now? (Max)*

Yes. Reading. (Red)

He knew she was probably somewhat annoyed with him for interrupting her book. It wouldn't be the first time.

> *I wonder if you'd still be able to read if I slipped my hand down your shorts? (Max)*

> *... (Red)*

> *... (Red)*

> *Would you want me to still be reading? (Red)*

She was catching on. He shifted a little uncomfortably in his seat, his hand briefly slid down over the semi-hardened state of his cock in his pants.

> *Noting the need to find out in the future. (Max)*

> *... (Red)*

> *Gah... (Red)*

Good, let her feel frustrated like he was too, Max thought.

> *Wanna play a game, Red? (Max)*

> *YES. (Red)*

Her fast response made him smile.

What the hell kind of game is that? (Red)

... ...

OH (Red)

Okay (Red)

Were they playing this game? Max heard the quiet internal voice questioning his judgment.

Max heard another internal voice remind him that Rose was an adult, already seemed somewhat familiar with Dominance and submission, and that at least he would be more protective of her than an unknown potential asshole might be. Dominant figures were a dime a dozen, especially since that popular book series hit mass market, but not all educated themselves or recognized their responsibility for protecting their submissive partners.

From themselves, if need be, the cautioning voice reinforced. *Look how well that's worked out,* the more fervent side of himself reminded.

Avoiding what was between them may have very well intensified things. It could be better to explore things and burn out the flames. *The accelerant could only fuel them for so long, right?*

He didn't get in until after 0130. He tried to remain quiet, but Rose had left her door cracked, and Luna came out to check on the commotion. She twisted between Buck's legs, and he sniffed her butt, kissing her nose once before going to lie down on his bed. Max smiled at her little clicking noises at him and scooped her up. He quietly took her back into the office, where Rose lay sleeping, her leg wrapped around the outside of the covers, the pillow over her head.

He gently dropped Luna on the bed, where she went to curl up next to Rose's pillow. He looked at Rose for a moment in the moonlight, gently running the tip of his finger up her leg, remembering all the times in his youth when he had wanted to do just that but didn't. Just like when he had been young, though, she slept like the dead and didn't move an inch.

He closed her door silently, not wanting to disturb her in the morning. There was still plenty of time for all that would be between them.

Chapter 7

Rose

Wednesday was busy. Rose had slept until nearly 9:30, rushing through her shower so she could have a little extra time to prepare before her class. She poured herself a cold cup of coffee that she knew was likely fresh today from Max's 5:30am rising time.

It wouldn't be the first time she'd drunk her coffee cold.

After her class was finished, she began to shuffle through her laptop bag, looking for her highlighter, when she noticed the stack of mail from the weekend that she hadn't gone through. Shuffling through the junk mail and throwing it in the trash bin under the desk, she noticed an envelope that didn't have a postal mark. Her name was written in neat, small handwriting, but no address. She slit the envelope open and pulled out a piece of general computer paper with only three words typed.

> *Stop digging, bitch.*

She dropped the paper.

What the hell? Was this connected at all to the bomb thing at the reception? It had to be. She took a quick picture with her phone and left it on the floor where she'd dropped it.

(Picture)

So this was in my mailbox Saturday. (Red)

Can you run by my place on your way home tonight and grab my mail? (Red)

Yep. Don't touch it anymore if you can help it. I'll be home in a few hours. (Max)

You okay? (Max)

Yes. The alarm is still set. (Red)

She'd checked the alarm as soon as she had texted him. She picked up Luna, who was sniffing the edge of the paper on the floor, which was in her domain, and shut the office door. She turned on some streaming music for some white noise and read to keep her mind from going insane. She'd never admit the breath she released when she heard the garage door open beneath her a few hours later.

Max and Buck walked in, the pup racing to her to sniff her hand and lick her reassuringly. Max walked straight to her and crouched in front of her on the couch, his hand immediately going to her cheek to encourage eye contact. She knew he wouldn't force it, but she lifted her eyes anyways as he gently stroked her cheekbone.

"You're okay," he said reassuringly, staying there for a moment as she drank in his strength. He reached down to squeeze her hand and then got up and went to the kitchen.

She got up and watched him pull some plastic gloves from a drawer and put them on, taking a gallon-sized plastic bag into the office as he picked up the letter from the corner and put it in the bag.

"The envelope," she gestured to the desk, where she had dropped the handwritten envelope. He added that to the bag as well, walking back to the living room and putting the plastic bag into his black leather messenger bag.

A weight lifted off her shoulders a bit as he zipped the bag closed, and she could no longer see the papers.

She released another breath.

He walked closer to her, her hands wrapped around herself protectively. He rubbed her arms and pulled her close. She laid her head on his chest, barely noticing his dress shirt and tie. "Why?" she asked. "Why would anyone want to hurt me?" She knew this likely meant the bomb had been related to her somehow.

And so many other people could have been hurt!

Max smoothed her curls back off her forehead. "Sometimes people are just shitheads, Rosebud," he told her soothingly in a low tone. "I've spent a lifetime trying to rationalize and understand people, and they just don't always make sense."

She let the nickname slide for now. Somehow when everyone else slipped back to calling her that, it was annoying but manageable. But with him, she didn't want to be a kid sister to him.

"I saw the chicken you were thawing. It's marinating now," she said quietly, pulling back a little.

"Okay," he responded, gently rubbing her back for a moment. "I figured we could sauté some vegetables or something with it." Luna jumped at his leg, using her claws to climb up his side. They separated, and he laughed as he scooped the kitten up with his hand and brought her to his chest to snuggle. Rose didn't blame the kitten for purring. She wanted to sometimes as well.

She shook herself a little and went into the kitchen. Pulling out the cutting board and knife from the strainer she had used for lunch, she got the squash she had seen in the fridge and began to slice it methodically for sautéing. Max turned the oven on to preheat the chicken breasts, pulling the bag they were marinating it in out of the fridge and prepared the pan while he waited.

They worked in companionable quiet while they made dinner, music streaming in the background. After eating and feeding Buck, Max tugged her by the hand until she tumbled onto the couch with him, tucking her into his arm in front of where he lay as he used the remote to scan for something to put on the television. For a while, they stayed just like that, Rose soaking up the strength of him behind her on the couch until she began to notice him hardening behind her.

Laying there, forgetting to watch what was happening on the tv with the drama episode he'd turned on, she hesitated to make a move, uncertain of what to do with her fuzzy thoughts. Teasing him just a little, she wiggled her ass closer to him, lining his cock up with her ass crack. She felt him smile a little against her neck as he began to nuzzle his short beard there, nipping at her ear.

His hand slowly rubbed up and down her side, down to her outer thigh where her soft shorts ended, and back up, sliding just beneath her tank to tease her softly on her lower ribs.

"So, how good were you last night, Red?" he asked her quietly near her ear. His hand slid around to cup her sex, sliding his middle finger along her center, hidden beneath her shorts.

"I... I... definitely didn't come... like you said," she said hesitantly. Not that she wouldn't have if she had wanted to, but she knew what waiting, when told, could do. How it could enhance the eventual orgasm. It was always her choice whether to listen or not. She knew that.

"But you did play a little bit?" he asked, his fingers continuing to lazily slide along the line of her pussy lips through her shorts. She squeezed her inner thighs together a little as her clit began to throb.

"Yes... a little..." she admitted, her breathing growing heavier.

"Show me," he said in her ear evenly, seeming to not be as affected as she was, but she knew he was. She could feel him behind her.

"Now??" she asked, her voice jumping an octave.

"Yes," he said, "Now." More commandingly, but still soft in her ear, his teeth a breath away from her skin. His hand returned to stroking her hip softly.

Not being able to look at him as he was behind her, she began to slowly run her hands down and then up her front as she might in her bed. Sliding her hands inside her tank strap, she pulled the top beneath her nipple, softly running her fingertips around the areola and then the budding nipple. She felt her breath hitch as she thought of him watching her over her shoulder, his hand resting at her hip, his thumb slowly stroking every now and then.

She pinched the nipple, at first softly, then quite a bit tighter, feeling the response in her throbbing clit. His breath deepened in her ear.

"Was that all you did Red? Or did you touch your little pussy?" he asked, his words like a direct stroke to her clit.

"I... I... I... did," She swallowed.

"Show me," he said unwaveringly, his fingers at her hip stilled, waiting.

She slid her hand softly down her ribs and soft stomach, sliding it inside her shorts and panties, her eyes slipping shut as she moved by sensation.

Her middle finger slid inside the lips of her vagina, stopping to softly stroke her most sensitive spot. She dipped her finger a bit lower, just entering the soaked canal. She stopped there, as that was where she had given up the night before in frustration. Taking her hand out of her shorts, he captured her wrist before she could wipe it on her shorts.

"Mmmmm... that was it?" he asked her. She nodded silently.

"Have you ever tasted yourself before, Red?" he asked, bringing her hand to her lips. His cock was thick, and she swore it was pulsing at her ass. She nodded her head, wondering if he would be surprised, but she felt him smile against her cheek as he said, "Show me," one more time.

Rose gingerly licked the tip of her middle finger, then sucked the full finger in her mouth, feeling what was happening behind her as his breath became more ragged. When she had finished, he growled as he climbed over her off the couch.

"As lovely as this couch has been for us, a bed would be better," he said, his hand out to help her up. Rose knew why he hadn't just pulled her up—he was offering her a decision. But she couldn't imagine doing anything else, so she took his offered hand as he pulled her to her feet. She followed him down the hallway to his bedroom.

He turned on the lamp next to the massive dark walnut, antique four-poster bed. The antique finder in her almost got derailed—it was so beautiful. But he picked her up by the waist and tossed her onto the gray quilt-covered bed. Rose laughed and turned over onto her back, leaning up on her elbows, her legs slightly parted. She met his eyes as he finished loosening his tie. He took it off, laying it neatly over the arm of the elliptical nearby, his shirt following almost methodically. Her breath caught in her throat as she looked at him, his tan chest tapering to his dress slacks, his cock tenting his pants.

"I want to get one thing out of the way, Red," he said, his eyes becoming serious. "We have skirted around this, but I think you are somehow familiar with kink. Am I right?"

She nodded slowly.

"You don't owe me details, but would you say you feel fairly experienced or a beginner?" His eyes strained at not asking for more, his jaw set tightly.

"One relationship, about a year-long, last year," she offered for now.

He took a breath and focused on her, his breath settling more naturally. "There is no relationship you could ever enter that removes your consent from you. Do you understand that Red?" he asked her, his eyes intent on her.

"I know that," she said matter of factly. "My grandfather taught me how to shoot a gun. I didn't forget."

Max laughed out loud. "Good. Good girl," he said, his finger slipping down her cheek to her chin. His thumb caressed her lower lip. "Do me a favor and shoot the hell out of anyone who makes you feel like you are less than they are, okay? There is no one like you, Rosebud." His eyes grew quiet.

"Red, yellow, green is how I play to keep it simple. If you have anything you'd rather use, feel free to speak up. We play safe, sane, and consensual. I don't do anything you don't want me to, and the same goes the other way. We must communicate what those mean to us, and we'll get to know those with each other as we go." He looked at her gently. "Don't forget to respond, okay? Especially if I check in with the colors."

After she nodded, he paused and thought for a moment, "We may need to reconsider the color red," he chuckled.

He walked to the head of the bed and slid open a rivet in the upper right post of the bed. Inside the hidden compartments on each side were soft, velvet red ropes attached. "You seemed responsive to my holding your arms the other day, Red. Is that something that interests you? Bondage?" he asked, watching her closely. She nodded, fascinated at the concept of this beautiful old antique bed being so kinky.

He crooked his finger at her.

She held out her left arm, quietly looked at him, and said, "Green, Max."

He held her gaze as he wrapped the soft crimson strap around her wrist and fastened it. He brought his lips softly to hers, their bodies barely even touching as he whispered, "Good girl. Now, lay down, please."

He walked around the grand bed, centered against the wall, getting rid of his socks and slacks as he did. He was left unabashedly in his black boxer briefs, contemplating her with a cocky grin. He stepped forward and secured her other wrist. She still had her clothes on, or at least the tank, panties, and soft cotton shorts she had changed into after lunch. He must have focused on that at the same time as he reached forward and slid her shorts and panties down her legs, leaving her in just the lacy tank top that did very little to hide her hardened nipples. At this point, she was so turned on that she couldn't have cared less if he had ripped it off her body and used it somehow. But he left it there, not seeming to worry about it, nor the leg straps she was sure must be hidden at the posts at the end of the bed.

"Now, little one, we see what happens to little girls who tease," he said, his eyes lit up with intent as he stripped his underwear and kneeled on the bed next to her. He smiled. "I couldn't help but imagine this as you licked your beautiful finger, Red," he said as he held his hard cock to her lips. Opening her mouth for him, she hungrily licked and sucked at what she could reach of his cock head.

But she wanted more and told him so. "Please... Closer, please..." she got out between reaching licks.

He moved, carefully kneeling over her with one leg on each side of her shoulders and slipped his cock back into her mouth, holding the top of the headboard to not put all his weight on her as he fucked her mouth.

"Damn, that pretty little mouth likes to be fucked, doesn't it, Red?" he asked her, not really seeking a response. But she nodded a little anyways, her hair wild like curly fire around her shoulders. Moving carefully, he reached down with one hand and filled his hands with her hair, cupping the side of her face, tugging gently as she gagged for a moment.

He backed up, leaning slightly on her chest, looking at her intently. *God, this kinky shit made her feel like a wanton whore, and she adored it.* Her breasts heaved with her panting, and she knew she had slobbered some when he fucked her face. But she felt sexy, and he was looking at her like he could eat her alive.

Backing back down her body, he settled for a moment at her waist, a knee to each side of her—somehow not putting all his weight on her. But the weight that was there felt good—grounding even, secure. He pulled her lacy-edged tank below her breasts, smiling to himself as he considered. Looking into her eyes, his fingertips trailed softly around her nipples.

"I have noticed that when you pinch your own nipples, you like it soft and then harder, Red. Am I right?" He smiled, his fingertips following his words as he pinched her pebbled nipples more roughly after the soft tracing. "You enjoy the alternate sensations, the oppositional reactions, don't you?" he said as she was already nodding, feeling his movements in her clit. He continued for a few moments until she was practically ready to beg him to fuck her.

"Max," Rose panted. "Please..."

Sitting back on his haunches on the bed, he just looked at her as he stroked his hard cock a few times. *God, what was taking him so long?*

"You are so goddamned beautiful, Rosebud," he said, his eyes returning to hers. He slid his hands along her legs, separating her thighs and pressing them back toward her chest. He nipped at her inner thigh as he moved in on her clit. His tongue stroked and flicked at her throbbing center.

Looking up at her, straining against the arm restraints, panting, he asked, "What do you want, Red?"

She moaned and writhed but didn't quite answer, unsure how to say what she was wanting. The line of communication between her brain and mouth seemed short-circuited by her wanting so badly to be fucked that she couldn't think straight. He slipped his middle and his forefinger along her wet slit from front to the tight little hole in the back and returned as he leaned up over her. That made her wriggle wildly as she began to try to move her legs against his leaning on them, but he jerked them back into place roughly, watching her closely.

"Check in with me, Red," his tone was serious.

"Green, green, I'm good," she panted. "Oh god, it's sooooo good…" she said as he circled her clit again with his middle finger. He turned his hand and slipped two fingers inside her, his thumb still slipping and circling her very wet clit.

He pressed against her legs, stretching her out like a gymnast, as he pulled his fingers out and rubbed his cock against her wetness, teasing her.

"Tell me what you want, baby," he said, leaning into her, his cock pressing against her, right where she craved him.

"Fu—fuck me, goddamnit!" Rose begged. "PLEASE."

With one swift movement, he entered her from behind her raised legs. "Fuuuuuck, Red," he groaned, pressing her legs farther back and his cock in even further. He slapped her ass lightly, and when she wiggled against him in response, he provided a soft, gentle stroke there and then slapped it a bit harder. Beginning to move, he ran his finger down her cheek, calling her attention to him. She opened her eyes, meeting his and holding as he began to fuck her, in and out, harder, faster as he pressed into her.

He slipped his thumb between them to slide just once against her clit, and almost immediately, she came, bucking wildly against him. He joined her just a few moments later, letting out a deep and guttural moan as skin slapped against skin, and they strained toward one another.

When she came back to her senses, his hands lazily ran up and down her thighs as they caught their breath. He slid his hand up her body, cupping the side of her face as he gave her a feather-soft kiss. Her legs fell to each side of him, her hips accepting the weight of him.

He pulled back again, leaning on one elbow as he lazily ran his hand down her body, cupping a breast and then trailing down her stomach to the short, trimmed strawberry hair of her pubic bone.

Reaching over to one and then the other, he released her restraints and pulled her into his lap as he settled against the majestic headboard. She sat facing him, hearing him groan as she felt him stir beneath her all over again, as their sexes touched in the seated position he had put her in.

"Jesus and fuck," he said, but she just smiled. I mean, she had been masturbating to the thought of him for years. She wiggled her ass on him, and he laughed, slapping her ass cheek.

"I can't get fucking enough of you, Red," he said quietly, gently pulling her wild curly head back. He tentatively felt the back of her scalp, searching for the place where the stitches had been. She took his hand and moved it to the spot behind her right ear, a little above her hairline.

"I'm being careful, but you have to tell me if I hurt your stitches in any way," he said, nodding once he seemed assured he hadn't. He leaned back against the bed and looked at her. He made her feel so sexy.

"I want to know the things you're into—the things you know you like and the things you're curious about," he said. She wasn't sure if he meant sex or hobbies or...

"Both," he laughed, guessing correctly again at what must have been the uncertainty he saw in her eyes. He had usually read her well back in the day too. He ran the tip of his finger down her nose. "Rose, I feel like I know so much about you, and yet there is so much I don't know."

She shrugged. "I'm a pretty open book."

He looked at her, his eyebrows raising, "About as open as I am."

She felt confused. She'd never tried to keep anything from him, at least not what he had been around for. Sure, he didn't know how bad things had gotten her junior and senior years, but he hadn't been there. She supposed he could say the same. He hadn't seemed to keep anything from her when she was around.

"Ask me a question then," Rose said, pulling the blanket up over her shoulders, feeling a little bit chilly but not wanting to leave his naked lap. She liked the feel of him against her softness.

He leaned back a bit and put a finger to his lips, looking at her. "Okay, what made you decide on the University of Texas? Was it to be close to family?"

"Yes," Rose answered, "And they offered me a scholarship, which was easier on my mother, who wanted to help pay for it." She looked at her hands for a moment and then looked him directly in the eye. "What made you decide on the Marines, and why then?"

He took a breath, pausing. "Honestly, Red?" he said, looking her in the eyes directly. "I was scared fucking shitless about all the feelings I had for you. Plus, my father was refusing to pay for the police academy. So, when Lieutenant Colonel Johnson said he could get me in the Marines if I left then for boot camp, I accepted. I had to get outta Dodge, Rose. I'm sorry if it hurt you." His eyes held hers for a moment until she got overwhelmed and looked away.

She swallowed. He *had* had feelings for her then. She wasn't sure what to think about all that.

"Okay, my turn," he said, shifting the focus as he tucked an errant curl behind her ear. "Top 3 things you enjoy about kink."

She blew some of her hair out of her face. "Top 3, huh? I must narrow it that much?" She laughed. "Okay. I like being told what to do when it's what I want to do. Especially when it's what I want to do, but I'm scared to do. It's helped with my anxiety some." He traced her chin thoughtfully. "Two, I like feeling sexy, and sometimes that's when I feel slutty." She blushed a little. "And I like to have my lines blurred a little, pushed just outside my comfort zone. I don't know, maybe all three of those are the same thing?" she resolved, throwing her hands up in the air.

He chuckled. "No, I can totally see those, Rosebud. They are very sexy," he said, his fingertip sliding along her neckline and circling a nipple that had been exposed from the blanket corner for a moment. He was already half hard against her thigh again.

"Okay," she said, "top 3 for you then." Looking at him, waiting for him to answer.

"Well," he said, pausing to think. "If I have to narrow to 3 as well, it would likely be watching someone explore their inhibitions—or the things they withhold themselves from but are secretly drawn to." He paused, thinking a moment before he spoke again, "Two would probably be bringing someone to orgasm, and then three would probably be the feeling of watching someone please me." He looked at her intently. "I know it probably sounds strange, but as much as I love the feel of soft lips on my cock, I love the sight and emotional aspect of the pleasing more."

He saw her yawn. Pulling her up with him by the pillows, he tucked her in the blankets next to him and turned off the light. "What's your plan for tomorrow?" he asked her quietly. "8am class?"

She nodded, noting that he remembered, and snuggled up against him. "I only have the two classes right now, one Tuesday and Thursday at 8, and then Monday, Wednesday, Friday at 11. You?"

"Last night was my biggest thing scheduled this week. Tomorrow, I had planned to mostly work from home and wrap up the paperwork. Friday, I will likely go in at least for the gym and a half day. Then I know we need to head out to Newheart and your family for the evening," he said quietly, as she was already falling asleep at his shoulder.

She felt Luna jump on the bed, mewling and looking for her. Finding her, she curled up on the other side of her, near the pillow.

Rose couldn't help but think, as she drifted off to sleep, that this was better than she could have ever imagined, but she hoped it didn't all fall apart just like it had before.

Chapter 8

Max

The next day went by smoothly. Max got up as normal and took Buck on a short run, returning to coffee and a half-awake Rose, who even smiled a bit as he pressed her into the island, kissing her neck from behind.

He showed her his shower, turning all three water streams on while Rose stood there in her tank top, and she yelped—whether from the cold water that initially sprayed across her front or his slap on her naked ass, he didn't know. But soon, the bathroom filled with steam as he finished waking her by removing her soaked tank and pulling her to stand between his legs as he sat on the bench, soaping her body and eventually turning her around to sit on his cock.

"Your little pussy likes to come for me, doesn't it, Red?" Holding himself back from orgasming too quickly at the extra tight entrance between her mostly closed legs as she lowered herself on his lap, nodding. He reached, slipping his finger between her pussy lips to stroke her clit, which he knew drove her wild. She leaned back against him as he stroked her wet breasts in the spray they were getting from the bench. It didn't take long, and they both quickly came together, the position heightening the sensations in the cascading water.

Rose kept her hair up in the ponytail bun she had put it in when she woke, letting him know that she would not be using his shampoo but that she would move hers in this shower if she was going to be using it regularly, as his shower was far better than the other bathroom he knew. But she did decide to soap him up, almost leading to more as he got out of the shower half hard again. He'd considered pressing her onto her knees right there in the spray, but he took pity on her hair and work situation.

Max's mother had often talked about her own natural curls and the difficulty of keeping them happy. He knew Rose and his mother's curls were different, his mother's being coarse and smaller. His momma had once told him that her's were a 4B and Rose's were a 3C, and that those were still pretty different. His mother had gotten on to Max early on when she heard he was teasing Rose by pulling on her hair. She reminded him that his own curls could be fussy in the Texas heat and that he knew better. All three Anderson brothers had curly hair actually. Jax and Max's curls were looser, but Nat's were tighter, closer to their mom's. Nat kept his hair short, his beard too. Max knew that was to avoid some of the talk that happened at times. Texas was Texas, even when you had money. That money shielded you some, but not completely.

Growing up in the 70's, especially in the South, his mother hadn't always had it easy, he knew. With a Black father and White mother, Lisette Anderson had faced ridiculously oppressive experiences in the South and had known about far worse from her parents' stories. When her father died young, her mother cleaned expensive homes to keep her and her daughter alive, and she had learned the lesson of hard work at too young of an age. But she had met a young, rich, Peter Anderson in Heartland's own high school and had fallen in love with the local Cattle Baron's son. It had taken a lot for his father to convince his mother to wed him and his legacy, but she had made sure her boys understood the privilege they carried from their wealthy family birthright. Above and beyond the financial and power privilege for the area, all three mostly passed for

White—especially Max, whose fairly loose curls needed little more than a soft cream to air dry. He knew the expensive cut he got helped as well.

But Lisette Anderson had raised her boys to be different from the financially powerful young people in Texas. They knew who they were—and the power they carried in humble fists. They were never too comfortable to get their hands dirty or to forget where she often reminded them she came from. Or to forget that there were some people who still existed who only treated them right because of their power in the community but talked about the boy's lineage behind their backs. The boys had had countless scuffles over their childhoods, with repetitive lessons from their mother about being better than the bigoted few. This all contributed to the impenetrable bond the brothers had, and no one messed with an Anderson brother—especially when they were together. They were always stronger together.

Max finished his paperwork by late afternoon and took a break to check in with Rose on some of the information he'd received the day before. He'd met with his uncle briefly on the way home and discussed the little bit that he knew about the pharmaceutical company that the traced call had come from. He had talked to a local precinct in New York, where their headquarters was reported to be, and they were going to do some local digging for him as well.

"What do you know about MidAtlantic Pharmaceuticals?" Max asked, sitting down in the easy chair as she was spread out on the couch with her laptop and some research materials. She looked up, taking off her tortoiseshell reading glasses.

Damn, she was hot in those glasses. Always had been. She seemed to mostly wear them for reading. He might need to ask her to make an exception one day, to wear them without her clothes on. He could almost imagine her riding him while still wearing them...

"Not too much, but I just stumbled across that name, actually," Rose said, looking at him inquisitively. "Why do you ask?"

Down, Anderson.

"Well, it seems to be where the number that called here the other night traces back to," he said. "We haven't been able to trace anything on the explosion yet, but I have feelers out on a few leads. I stopped by and talked to my uncle yesterday on the way home, thought I might pick his brain on the company. He mentioned they are a mass production company and that they have a new blood pressure medication that he's aware is getting ready to go to market, which has gotten some curious negative feedback in the past." He rubbed his lower lip, thinking for a moment.

"Well, ironically, they are the manufacturers of a commonly prescribed medication for anxiety related to trauma as well. I was reading about it in the article released last week on the newest study of neurotransmitter activity involved in trauma reactions," Rose commented. "But what would they want with me?"

"I mean, they called my house, remember?" Max responded. "But they shouldn't really have anything they want from me. But how they figured out you were here, I don't know. I called a few favors in, as they are headquartered in New York. Maybe a few of my connections up there can find something out."

Rose looked disturbed, going back to her tracking. "Why the hell would anyone want to harm medical research that helps people?" she asked, looking up.

"People find all kinds of strange reasons to intimidate in the business world, Red. Usually, it's fear that it might affect the bottom dollar, or hiding something, or even just fear of the unknown," he said. She'd put her glasses back on, reading the screen again. *Dammit, those fucking glasses.* He used to fantasize about pushing her up against some library shelf and having his wild way with her.

Why couldn't he get enough of her? Craving her was definitely not abating. He needed some self-control.

He decided to work on dinner, giving her more time to work. After they finished eating, he turned on the news to catch up on things while they worked together to clean the kitchen. She yawned a few times as they finished, so he pulled her onto the couch again to actually snuggle, setting a goal for himself to let her relax as they continued the new drama series they had started the night before.

It wasn't long before she fell asleep, curling towards him and into his neck, her soft breath against his skin. He gave himself a moment to consider what life might be like if they were to continue this as a real relationship after everything returned to being safe for her. The thought of it all ending made it hard to breathe, so he pushed the thought out and forced himself to focus on the show.

It would work itself out in time. He hoped. With, at a minimum, Rose unscathed.

Rose

She didn't even remember going to bed the night before but woke in the morning to her watch alarm at 9am, alone in Max's bed. She knew she slept hard most of the time, but she must have been tired if she didn't remember him carrying her to bed or his stripping her down to her tank to sleep. Laying there, she ran her hands over her body for a moment, imagining him taking her clothes off her. She really needed to pick up her vibrator from her apartment. So instead, she took a sexyish morning selfie, avoiding most of her face and tugging her lacy tank top down for deep cleavage and a bit of areola showing.

Welllll, look who's finally awake. (Max)

Mornin Red (Max)

That's a lovely way to interrupt my day, thank you Ma'am. xo (Max)

I'm sure we could work something out. (Max)

You might enjoy checking out the bottom drawer of my dresser for now. (Max)

She immediately scooted to the edge of the bed and slid onto the floor next to the drawers. She'd figured he had some things but didn't want to dig. Pulling out the shallow bottom drawer, she saw all kinds of leather items and dug until she found a small wireless pocket vibe and checked the power. Finding it working, she took a picture of her lips kissing it.

I see that (Max)

Ummmm can I use it?? Please? (Red)

...

...

I think you should have to earn it first. (Max)

Hmmmm okay. How could I do that? (Red)

...

...

No panties tonight at your family dinner, and wear a skirt, please. (Max)

10-4 Danno. (Red)

(Max)

She had just enough time to shower, washing her hair in Max's fantastic shower. She hadn't brought many options for clothing but had thrown in a short jean skirt, so she wore that with a black lacy tank and a cropped thin white sweater and planned to wear her cowboy boots. For now, she wore her panties, as she taught her class at 11am, but she did plan to remove the specified article of clothing in time for dinner.

Max got home around 1pm and she mentioned hoping they could leave within the hour and stop in town in Newheart. He took a quick shower while she fed Buck, as they'd decided to leave the pets home for the evening. She was pulling on her boots when he came out, dressed in jeans and a blue and gray button-up appropriate for dinner on the Ranch with her family, his thick curls wet and slicked back for now and freshly shaved. She was going to miss that scruff.

He pulled on his boots, and they headed out. It wasn't long into the drive before he asked her if she had left her panties behind.

"No, not yet." She blushed. "You said dinner, right? I thought I'd see Kitty first."

"I meant the whole damn night, darlin'," he drawled quite firmly. "If you are interested in this sweet little thing," he took out the small pocket vibe from his shirt pocket and twirled it in the air, catching it easily despite driving, "I need something in return."

"Now??" she asked, feeling her heart race as they drove in the Explorer down the busy four-lane highway in rush hour traffic headed east out of town.

"Yes, ma'am," he said. "I guess you'll get creative, won't you?" Smirking, he glanced over to traffic on her side as he merged a lane in the steadily moving traffic out of town.

Looking around, immediately turned on but not wanting to be seen, she inched her skirt up a little at a time from her thighs where the hem rested. She took a breath and inched it up a little more, reaching her fingers to hook her fingertip over the edge of the lace, knowing the very tip of her panties showed a little bit beneath the skirt edge if anyone were to look down into the vehicle. Only a few vehicles would have been tall enough, really, like the truck they suddenly passed to their left. She knew she could jerk down the skirt, but she would have to start all over again, or she could just get it done, so she shimmied her way out of the panties, sliding them down her legs and over her boots.

She set the panties on the seat between them.

"Good girl," he murmured low, the sound sliding along her spine like a caress, and she wanted to purr in response. He pocketed her panties and laid his hand on her left thigh, his pinky finger sliding dangerously close to the bottom edge of the skirt. But he didn't touch higher, just remaining close, reminding her he could if he wanted to as he drove.

"I know we have at least another hour, so I sent you something to your personal email right before I left. You could fill that out for me if you want to," he said, turning the music up a little bit as he settled in for the ride.

She pulled her glasses out of her purse pocket and opened her email, clicking on the link he had sent her. Up popped a secure page for kink-interested individuals, where she actually already had an account. She doubted he knew that. She peered at him through her lashes and glasses. He'd sent her a quiz link regarding her experiences, interests, and limits. When she clicked on it, it opened the quiz under her account. It immediately popped up and asked if she wanted to be friends with DominantDallasBronco, who had sent her the link, and she held back a giggle at the name.

"So, I have an account on there," she said quietly. "I made it at some point last year."

"Makes sense," he said quietly. "I guess you found the quiz?"

"Yes." She nodded. She'd done something like it for her last Dominant as well. She appreciated the intentional communication and not assuming he could always read her mind. She began to select some of the answers, flushing a bit as she thought about it. She knew a few things had changed since a year ago, a few she had learned she didn't like, and a few she was more curious about now.

She knew connecting on the site allowed Max access to see some of the photos she had added the year before. Exhibitionism, within reason, definitely turned her on. Filling out the damn quiz was turning her on. Not wearing the panties when she was taking Max home with her turned her on.

That reminded her... She took a deep breath.

"So, I think we agree that no one needs to know about, you know, us and whatever this is that we are doing?" she asked awkwardly. *How do you even say that?* They weren't really dating. They hadn't been on a single date. They were having sex while he was protecting her, and you didn't just tell your family that.

He kept his eyes trained on the road. "Right. So, just like we are friends?" He moved both hands back to the steering wheel as he turned left onto the old road that led to Newheart.

"Friends who feel like family even," she responded, unsure why things suddenly felt so cold.

"Right," he said, turning the music back up a little and focusing on the road.

Rose had driven this route hundreds of times since leaving for college. She could have almost done it blindfolded, and she imagined Max could too. But suddenly, she felt like she needed to watch the road as moments from the past flitted through her mind, flashing from years back in high school as well as the last few days.

The emotions there were real. She had to push them back down.

Chapter 9

Rose

Newheart, Texas had less than 8500 people. It was a small town where people often considered that there were more cattle than humans, and that didn't even count the chickens. The town center couldn't have been more quaint with its small central park with the antique but carefully and safely maintained playground filled with children and the small rustic train running year-round at its perimeter every Monday through Saturday by old Mr. Harper, who was old enough to be retired but refused to, enjoying the happiness the train brought to the children of the town.

Surrounding the town center were businesses on all four sides of the park square. Maine and Newheart Lane were the small town's initial cross streets before the park was added decades ago. The Coffee Corner, where Rose begged to stop first, was next to Kitty and Kendall's Klip & Kurl. She wanted a lavender iced tea first before sitting down to chat with her best friend. The High School had already let out, and the Primary School was just now releasing, so the quaint little coffee shop was bustling with teens flirting and doing homework. Rose patiently waited for her drink while Max checked in on his emails from his phone while they waited. Max had insisted he wasn't leaving her until she was settled at Kitty's shop despite Rose telling him she would likely be fine in Newheart.

Newheart was the safest place she had ever known. Rose had moved there when she was almost too young to remember "the before" anymore—or before her father had died. What she did remember was that she had much preferred the small town where her grandparents lived and the quiet small country school, to the loud and busy schools she'd attended in Dallas beforehand. Rose had liked it so much better that, for a while, her younger self had carried guilt, thinking that preferring to be there might have contributed somehow to her father's death.

For a quiet, severely introverted first grader like Rose, she had struggled to make friends in a big city. But here, in Newheart, Kitty had taken her under her wing from day one, despite being a year ahead of Rose. She had found Rose on that first day at lunch, commented on the book Rose had been carrying when nervously looking for a place to sit by herself to eat, and then chattered at Rose for the rest of the lunch hour over a hostess cake—which she had offered to share.

Thank god for small schools that let the grades sit wherever they wanted at lunch. Rose hadn't been able to talk to anyone in her class, her teacher included, for the first few weeks.

Rose didn't talk to Kitty either at first, but Kitty almost hadn't needed her to. Later, Rose learned that Kitty had ADHD, or Attention Deficit Hyperactivity Disorder, and as a natural extrovert she could pretty much talk to anyone—even when they were young. But Rose hadn't felt like just anyone. Kitty made her feel special and like she was talking only to her. Kitty had brought bows for Rose's hair the second week, showing Rose how to braid the kinky, curly hair they had in common. Kitty had then been the first person Rose had eventually talked to, before even her family... after her father's death. It had only been a word here and there, but Kitty had never acted differently. Never expecting more and never making a big deal of Rose's silence. And, of course, over time, Rose had slowly warmed up more, and Kitty could even get her going on certain topics by the time they were in their preteens.

Kitty had been her person growing up. She may have been what saved Rose at six years old. Not that Rose had ever told her that. That was too much for a then 7-year-old Kitty to be responsible for.

Sometimes Rose missed her when living in Dallas, but it wasn't too hard to text, or video chat, or even visit each other. Not really. They both were pretty busy with their work, but they stayed connected. They made it fine through the time Kitty was in Houston for college.

Max walked her to the Klip & Kurl. He'd be back after he said hello to Nat, who was currently working out at Boxing Boyz, the gym on the other side of the park on 2nd Street that their old high school PE teacher owned. Smack between Jenson's old Auto Parts and Salvage Repair and the Newheart Bank, the gym was much rougher than the one at the Community Center on Newheart Lane. That one was more family-friendly, and the one out at the old Country Club and Golf Course was where the ritzier folks went. Rose had only ever been into Boxing Boyz once, and that was way back in high school when she had been looking for Mr. Rogers to sign some papers for school to finalize her PE credit her senior year. All she remembered was it smelled like sweat and antiseptic, and was noisy, with loud music and the constant sound of folks in the old boxing ring in the center, the clang of metal now and then from the weights being lifted and dropped at the outer circumference of the room. Rose had never been a weight-lifting kind of person, preferring swimming and hiking if anything.

Kitty was in the middle of trimming the elder Mr. Roger's hair, in fact, when Rose entered the Klip & Kurl. The buzz of the razor over the older Black gentleman's head didn't stop Kitty from chattering away as she lined the trim of the salt and peppery dark hair around his ears, moving on to trim his more-pepper-than-salt beard next. Mr. Rogers looked nothing like the famous Mr. Rogers ironically, as even in his late 60's, he remained buff and tall. Rose couldn't imagine him wearing Keds and a cardigan, hiding a giggle at the thought. But he did have on his classic whistle, worn every day when they were in school. He wore it at the gym even back then too. Nowadays, he was retired from the school district but maintained the gym, supporting some of the school wrestlers in their developing skills, as well as the rest of the would-be boxing men in the neighborhood trying to avoid the beer bellies of age.

Kitty finished up, popping a quick kiss to the older man's weathered cheek. She called it "soft as a baby's bottom" after the homemade oil and soap lather she had used, likely shaving him before Rose had walked in.

"Well, hello there, young Miss Rose," the gruff voice of her former teacher greeted her with a smiling wink as he gathered his famous older boxing jacket from the nearby pearl hook. "Staying in town long?"

"No, sir," Rose answered him, never having forgotten his kindness in school as he would not force her, nor make a big deal about, participating in touch-based athletics like wrestling or tag football, allowing her to run solitary laps if she preferred around the old football stadium for her PE credits.

"Just in town for family dinner tonight. Momma cooks on Fridays and says we all gotta be here when we can," she explained. "I'm just stopping in to check on Kitty. The shop is really starting to come together, isn't it?"

Kitty had worked for the old barber, Mr. Jackson, all through high school, starting even earlier than most at their first job. She had talked the older gentleman into letting her sweep after his cuts for cash under the table when she was only 13. She had always loved doing hair, and Mr. Jackson was the closest they had in Newheart to a real salon growing up, most women at the time drove into Dallas for their cuts and colors. When Mr. Jackson, who had no known family that anyone knew of, had died unexpectedly of a heart attack while Kitty was gone to college, the old storefront had stood empty for years. Kitty had eventually convinced Kendall to go into business with her and reopen the shop as a one-stop hair and barbershop, as they had both learned a great many tricks growing up for hair, including cutting and coloring friends' hair in their teenage years when begged. They had opened almost a year ago, but they were still slowly renovating.

Rose sat in the aqua-colored, leather swinging chair next to where Mr. Rogers had been sitting as Kitty swept from the recent trim. Mr. Rogers tipped the ball cap that he settled on his freshly trimmed and edged hair and swung out the door, the old chimes singing as he whistled his way down the street.

"GIRL," Kitty started right away. "This place has been hopping. I tell you what!" Rose could hear Kendall's irritable muttering as she moved some things around in the back office.

"Don't mind her," Kitty muttered. "Something done crawled up her ass lately, but I think it's that Reggie is an asshole, and she seems to be realizing it, so that's a good thing." She shrugged it off as easily as she did everything else.

"What do you think about the new wallpaper?" Kitty chattered on about the renovations. Rose knew it was a slow remodel due to limited funds for the sisters. Two years apart, they couldn't have been more different. Kitty was light-hearted, fun, and generally excited about life. Kendall, as the oldest, had always been much more focused and responsible and took things much more seriously. Sometimes too serious for Kitty, as she would often complain to Rose.

If Kendall hadn't been three years older than Rose, they might have been much more likely to be friends than she and Kitty. Rose had always felt they were a lot alike. No, Kendall didn't seem to struggle as much as Rose to fit in with people—Kendall drew people to her like a beacon. They trusted her and looked to her for guidance. She had received a full-ride scholarship to a prestigious historically Black university in Houston that would have likely been too expensive for her to afford. Rose figured Kendall could have done anything with the business degree she graduated with, but she was here, running the business side of the sisters' new venture. Rose always wondered how Kendall felt about that.

The new wallpaper Kitty was still talking about had thick black and white lines with thin aqua-colored dashes in between them, the look contributing to the feminine, modern take on an old-school barbershop. The six swinging aqua and chrome vintage barber chairs lined in front of the half wall of mirror, Rose knew, had to have cost them a pretty penny. Rose definitely hadn't been rich growing up, but Kendall, Kitty, and their mother had struggled at times, she knew, especially after their father disappeared.

Kitty saw Rose stroking the leather softly and drawled in response, "Yes, ma'am. Those chairs sure are purdy, aren't they? I knew they would be worth every single penny. I knew I had to have them with the last of the loan money for the building renovation. The rest will come in time. I have two teal striped barbershop poles coming though, for outside the front door," she squealed. "UGGH, I can't wait!" And she did a little dance around the room with her broom.

Kitty finished sweeping and plopped herself down in the chair next to Rose, swinging to face her.

"Now tell me," she said, her voice dropping to a stealthy tone. "How are things going with Max? Have the two of you...?" She wiggled her eyebrows suggestively, smiling broadly.

Rose blushed but was saved from answering as Max took just that moment to stride in the door. All Rose could suddenly think about was being sans panties under her short jean skirt. She clenched her thighs together slightly, which only reminded her that it turned her on a bit. Max winked at her, noticing from behind Kitty before she turned to greet him.

"Maxwell Anderson," Kitty beamed at him. "Well, if you aren't more handsome than ever, I swear. When are you gonna trust me with those curls of yours?" she teased him, knowing he went to some fancy salon in Dallas. "You know, I cut your Momma's hair now."

Max raised his eyebrow, considering for a moment. "Well. I do trust my Momma's hairstylists." He sat down in one of the chairs and swung himself towards the mirror, winking at Kitty and nodding. Kitty squealed, rubbing her hands together excitedly.

Max laughed, "Now Katherine Mayfield, don't you go doing anything drastic. Just a dusting, please." He winked at Rose in the mirror as Kitty tightened her apron. *Damn, he'd always been a charmer.*

Kitty smiled broadly at him as she pulled out her antique scissors and sharpened them all too excitedly. "I got you, sir. No worries. No new styles today."

Kitty began to spray water to wet his curls and combed his hair with her fingers as she played around with Max's hair, deciding where she wanted to start. Max's eyes settled on Rose in the mirror, burning a hole straight to her clit, she swore, as she wiggled a bit in her seat.

Max's eyes remained on hers, twinkling, as his lips settled into a firm line, trying not to smile. She knew that he knew what she was thinking. *Damn him and his early push of the task. Maybe she didn't need that vibrator so much... Yes, she did.* She crossed her legs, knowing full well what he caught a glimpse of in the mirror. Thankfully, Kitty was busy chattering away about the time she spent in Houston training under some rich entrepreneur in his then up-and-coming hair salon and how famous he had become now.

All Rose could pay attention to was the heat between her thighs. She swallowed a cool drink of her lavender mint tea to soothe her parched throat.

"I see Rose got herself some of that fru-fru iced tea over at Ms. Lola's," Max teased, lightening things a bit. "How is she and Ms. Julia?" he asked Kitty and Rose both, pronouncing the latter with the natural H sound as they had learned growing up. Texas had a strong Latin and Mexican heritage running through it, and Newheart was no different. Newheart prided itself on diversity and sought to make its small town a safe haven for any who settled there over the years, thanks to early founders. There were still some now and then who showed their ugly side, but Rose didn't often think that lasted very long. But she knew she wasn't the one who experienced it most when it did, not like her best friend and Max and his brothers.

Kitty filled them in on the long-term partners over at the coffeehouse. The older couple had been together longer than the three could remember. Ms. Lola would often read the tea leaves and loved nurturing the community, while Ms. Julia was more the business person behind it all, running things like they were a Navy ship, a sign of her time in the Navy as a nurse when she was younger. The coffeehouse had always been a safe place for young people in town to hang out and get help with homework, as Ms. Lola had been a teacher before she retired and opened the Coffee Corner.

"Believe it or not, they started a Karaoke night on Friday nights and stay open later," Kitty exclaimed. "If I could sing, you know I would so be there. But alas..." She stepped back, assessing her work on Max as she put away the trimmer she had used to clean up his sideburns.

"Maxwell, that is one fine head of hair you have there, sir. I wish my curls were as naturally loose as yours." Kitty smiled in appreciation. "Thanks for giving me a chance. I hope I passed the test." She looked at him anxiously, eyes wide.

Max ran his hands through his collar-length curls, nodding his head and smiling at Kitty. "Well, I guess I have a new place to get my haircut when I'm home. Thanks Kitty!" Getting out of the chair, he kissed her cheek affectionately. They had all run in similar circles back in the day. Rose sometimes forgot what it had been like to be together with so many people she knew and felt comfortable with.

Max pulled out his leather wallet and began to shuffle through the bills when Kitty looked up from her sweeping. "Nah, Max, just keep your money. We'll call this a trial run. Next time you get to pay, and you best bring a tip." She smiled, winking instead at Rose, who was unsure what that even was for.

"You need to come to stay at the house again soon, girlfriend, after all this mess is cleared up in Dallas," Kitty said seriously to Rose as she walked them to the door and held it open. "It's been too long, for sure! Max, you keep my girl safe, ya hear? Text me! Byeeeee!" She knew Kitty likely stood at the door and watched them walk to the Explorer, parked on the side of the street. She knew Kitty didn't miss Max's hand at her lower back as he opened the door for her to get in and hoped she'd write it off as his Momma raising him right.

She knew she'd find out eventually, either way when Kitty texted her later after work.

Thankfully, they pulled up to the Montgomery Ranch before too long, and Matthew was just walking back to the house from the barn, likely finishing for the afternoon. She saw a few high school boys who helped out on the farm taking off on a shared truck, down the barn and around the back road over to their neighboring property.

Max pulled the Explorer up to the side of the barn to park, where he must have countless times in the past. Walking around to her door, he opened it for her again. Noting her nervous look at her brother, he stated quietly that he would have anyways, no matter who she was to him.

"Need I remind you, ma'am, if I hadn't stood here for a moment, you would have flashed your naked little pussy at your brother," he said, his voice low and slow, as he trailed his finger up her thigh and stroked the line between her labia briefly, all hidden behind the open dark window and door of the Explorer. He smiled slowly, like a cat who found the cream. "And so wet for me, too..."

Her eyes were wide as she forgot to breathe for a second, but she pulled her shit together as her mother came out the door and called a greeting to them. Max grinned even wider but stepped back just enough for her to slide out of the tall vehicle without flashing her family, and they made their way to the porch.

Max and Matt connected, a brotherly hug between them, immediately picking up on chatting about the ranch and the changes he was already starting. Her grandmother was in the kitchen working on dinner, and the table was already set for all five of them. Her mother had somehow had no doubt that Max would come with her, what with the additional place already set at the table.

Was it not obvious to others that they had avoided each other for the last 11 years? How could they all act like this was so normal when in all actuality, it was the very opposite? She felt the emotion rising up in her and tried to compress it back down. Her wet clit also noticed when he entered the room, thanks to his dare or whatever it was. She blew an errant curl off her forehead. Whatever—he'd barely looked at her twice since they'd arrived.

He was clearly far better than she was at playing this game of not being attracted to each other.

She stirred her grandmother's Irish beef stew, tasting it. Two warm home-made bread rounds rested on the back of the stove. She still remembered when her grandmother would make homemade bread so many years ago, one of the first memories she had of the ranch at 6, when they had just moved out here after their father had died. Everyone was anxious about Rose not talking, but not her grandmother. The way the family told the story was that it was over endless loaves of rising bread that she was able to connect with Rose, and eventually, she began to slowly talk at home again. Rose had never added the part about Kitty helping. She knew she had used rare words with her friend at school before she had at home, but the guilt she had carried at the time, over literally everything, had weighed her down so much it was as if she hadn't been able to speak through the mud in her throat.

She moved to the table as the stew was being served, the seat left open for her across from Max, who sat next to Matthew, and she sat next to her momma. Her grandmother sat at the head of the table now, where her grandfather had once sat for so many years. Her thick Irish accent slipped in now and then when she didn't overly think about it too much.

Underneath the table, Rose felt Max's boot slip between hers, at first just resting there patiently. After about ten minutes or so, when she had nearly forgotten, she almost choked on her stew when she felt his boot suddenly inch hers over a bit, separating her legs a few inches.

She coughed, covering up the moment, but she knew that he knew as he smiled into his spoon of thick beef and potatoes. Deciding she could give as well as she got, she slid the toe of her boot up his calf and along his inner thigh for a moment until he suddenly gripped the toe of the boot without moving an inch. She hadn't even known he had one hand beneath the table, but when he didn't let go right away, she had to cover her laughter with another cough, and her grandmother commented that she had better watch that cough.

"Yes, ma'am, I will. Excuse me, though. I need to use the restroom," she said, as her mother began to gather dishes to start to clean up, and Matthew mentioned finishing the last of the chores for the night, excusing himself to the barn to help their few remaining staff who were finishing up for the night.

She escaped to the second floor, where there was a bathroom next to her old bedroom, fanning herself with her hand as she closed the door, thinking about how she had survived dinner in her pantyless state. The sun was just setting outside the window, so she didn't even turn the light on as she looked out at the property for a moment. She missed the peacefulness of the country sometimes. She nearly jumped out of her skin when she felt strong hands slide around her from behind but smelled his aftershave as his cheek came to slide against hers.

"SHIT. I didn't even hear you open the door..." she bit back the yelp and tried to whisper.

"Shhhhhhh..." he cautioned, his hands slowly hiking up her short skirt. His middle finger immediately found her wetness and slipped between her vaginal lips, sliding against her clit once and then twice as she gasped.

He slipped a hand over her mouth, reminding her in her ear that her family would hear if they weren't careful, the bathroom door still cracked open in the darkening room. He slid a hand into her curls at the crown of her head, away from her mostly healed stitches, and pulled her by her hair over to the long bathroom counter, leaning her forward over it, her face close to the darkening mirror where she could see herself, her mouth open with her heavy breath, his dark shape behind her in the shadows.

He slid her skirt up and over her ass, roughly rubbing her wet pussy from behind. She bit her lip to not beg aloud. She had no clue who these sexy people were in the mirror, but they were damn sexy. On fire in her lover's grip from behind her.

Max slid his zipper down, his other hand still in her hair as she arched her ass towards him. He stroked his cock head against her wetness, wetness she knew had been there for much of the afternoon and early evening. Max pushed quickly, pulling her hips towards himself, and she gasped a little louder than she probably should have.

His hand came up to cover her mouth, and she licked him, biting gently. Not afraid of her teeth, he kept his hand right there to muffle her sounds as he began to fuck her from behind in the dark bathroom, quickly and roughly. Anyone could come at any moment, and it heightened the intensity. He began to pound into her faster and faster, and she watched her wanton self in the mirror as she ran her hands up underneath her sweater, twisting furiously at her own nipples through her lacy tank. She felt his other hand find her clit and she mewled into his hand as she almost immediately came. He grunted, barely containing the noise as he finished in her with his final thrust, both of his hands going to her hips to strain against her the one final time—pressing her firmly against the mirror, her cheek pressed against the mist from her gasping breath.

"I cannot tell you how many times I imagined doing that my senior year to your little teenage cunt," he whispered huskily in her ear as he quickly pulled out of her and zipped his jeans like he had just used her and was moving on. *God, that was hot.* He slid her skirt down and turned her around, meeting her eyes in the darkness. She knew he must have glanced over her list as he added darkly, "Now your cunt is mine, whenever, wherever, little one." He traced a fingertip down her jaw.

"Good girl, you've earned this." He took the small pocket vibe out of his pocket and slipped it into the pocket of her jean skirt. She would end the evening with it in her pocket, hoping the shape wouldn't be noticeable to family, nor the smell of him on her, dripping from her really, being without panties and all to catch what remained of him inside her. He silently slipped out of the bathroom, and she took a moment to clean herself up as best as she could and addressed her tousled hair.

Her mom talked them into staying for a few rounds of cards. No one seemed to pick up on anything between them that she was aware of, and Rose didn't push any secret flirting with Max, despite not being against a redo. Other than him calling her Red a few times, which no one seemed to think anything of, he really was much better than she at playing unaware. She just stayed quiet, which she counted on not being completely unusual for her.

She thought about the fact that Max had admitted to having sexual fantasies about her his senior year when she had started crushing on him so hard and how what they had just done was so much better than what she had fantasized about, rubbing herself late at night as a teen, or humping her pillow silently after dark.

For a brief moment, she imagined what life would have been like if they had explored that then and were maybe sitting around the table as a couple with her family right now... But then they both wouldn't be who they were now. They probably would have stayed in Newheart and never accomplished their current lives. Sitting with these feelings of no regrets was interesting for her, as she'd often regretted not completing what they had started the night of her sixteenth birthday. Now, knowing that he *had* wanted her all those years ago shifted something inside her.

In the dark on the long ride home, she remained quiet, uncertain of what to do with the various connections her mind was making. Keeping their sex compartmentalized was necessary to her, or this warmness that was expanding inside would get too many expectations, too much hope.

His thumb rubbed lazy circles against her outer thigh as he drove, not interrupting her silence. At one point, he turned up the music, the heavy rock filling her brain and pushing her thoughts to the edge for now. Maybe he had needed something to silence the thoughts too. He slipped his fingertip inside her pocket and pulled out the vibe, turning it on low and silently sliding it between her legs in the dark car, the drums thumping the bass in the vehicle's sound system.

"Don't... Come..." he said simply, the vibe placed against her clit in the darkness. They rode the rest of the way home that way, his thumb returning to lazy circles against her leg every now and then, the vibrator slowly working her into a wet frenzy all over again as the last minutes of the drive took unusually longer than felt normal. All thought but orgasming now fully gone from her overworked mind by the time he parked, and she heard the garage door closing.

They sat still in the dark vehicle, the car turned off, but the music still played loudly. He seemed to contemplate what he wanted to do for a moment, and then he unsnapped her safety belt and pulled her to kneel over him right there in the car, hitting the button to slide his seat back a bit, giving them more room. He unzipped his pants, and she immediately slid down on his cock, both moaning as he held the vibrator in place on her clit and against his cock. She had already been so close, riding the edging of the vibe, that she immediately began to pulsate with her first orgasm, her skirt up around her waist.

He wouldn't let the vibrator off her sensitive clit, though and the first wave of orgasm wasn't too long followed by a second as he slid both of her shirts up, pulling her bra beneath her breasts and pinching her nipples tightly between his fingertips. She rode him as he came, groaning into her neck as he bit down against her skin gently.

"Fuuuuckkk Red," he ground out, gripping her hips and pounding her down harder on his cock, until he finally thrust one final time into her.

She panted, spent, against his chest, still feeling him inside her for the second time tonight in the dark.

"Fuck, baby, I knew we weren't going to make it upstairs before I had to feel your throbbing mess on my cock," he said throatily as he kissed her forehead. His thumbs circled soothingly on her thighs, his forehead came to rest against hers. "Sometimes I wonder if this would be as intense as it is between us if we had explored things when we were younger?"

"Maybe we weren't who we needed to be yet then," she said simply, finding his eyes in the dark vehicle as the music surrounding them timed out. Her thighs felt like jello, but she made it back into her seat, collecting her panties and the vibrator.

That night she slept like the gods had blessed her—deep and peaceful and dark, her dreams filled with images of dark figures and sex and vulnerable intimacy.

Chapter 10

Max

The next week seemed to go by without a hitch to Max. Nothing unusual happened that threw either of them off. Rose seemed to question if he was worried specifically about her over nothing, as he hadn't found a direct link to the pharmaceutical company and Rose, other than the calls the one night, but his gut told him to wait it out. He trusted his gut.

Over the previous weekend, they had relaxed, running by Rose's place to pick up a few things, and getting her own car. She parked the red—of course, it was red—little Honda in the visitor section of the lot, as she was hoping to be able to get out a little bit this week. He had given her the passcode to the gate to enter as a visitor, so she could come and go as she pleased. Max had just asked that she let him know when she went somewhere in case anything happened. He would at least know where she last was.

Sex between them stayed pretty intense, despite his expecting it to die down. But they had found a routine, and he wondered how he would eventually let her go back to living in her tiny apartment, so close and yet so far from him, with her cheap-ass security system. At least that was what he told himself was the reason.

He'd never wanted to come home so much in the evenings before, not like he did now.

His parents had asked him to come over for dinner this Friday, and since it had been a while, he agreed but mentioned he would have Rose with him, as he was still looking out for her until they knew more. His parents had always seen Rose as his younger sister through Matt, so he had mentioned it to Rose, and she informed her mother that they wouldn't make it to the Montgomery ranch this weekend.

For a brief moment, he wondered if this was what it would be like if things had worked out from the beginning, trading off weekends with their families. But he roped *that* thought in before it roamed on into more dangerous territory.

Instead, he wondered if he could talk Rose into some sexy option like the week before and then down into his old bedroom where his teenage fantasies of her had gone wild. From naked on the back of his horse with him to joining him in his shower, teenage him had jacked off to fantasies of Red more than he would ever probably admit. They hadn't ended even after he left home, either. There had been a few redheads along the way that he'd tried to connect with, but it had just never been the same. Eventually, he had started to avoid dating redheads, as all they did was remind him that they just weren't her and all he had ever been was discontent.

Max had looked over her Kinkster account a few times since the other night. He'd had to be careful to not spend too much time thinking about it, or he found himself feeling possessive of her, and she wasn't his, not really. They hadn't discussed a relationship, and he felt it unfair to consider bringing it up when her life might be in the balance for now. She had a dozen or so photos on there, some selfies and some that had been taken by someone else. He could sense that she felt empowered by the sexy photos, and he truly was happy she had found that within herself. He'd found her list of experiences versus interests and limits interesting, often lining up with his. He smiled, knowing they had checked off "sex in an unknown, dark place" a few times for her now, with some mild exploration already of her exhibitionist interests.

Max wanted to be the one that introduced her to the rest. Who guided her in the continued exploration of her sexuality. But for now, they were limited to what things were until he knew she was safe. Then maybe they could discuss the rest.

Friday, he went in early to the gym and pumped some iron. He preferred to put his earbuds in and ignore everyone else, so he built up a sweat and tried not to think about fucking Red in his boyhood bed that night. It halfway worked, but by the time he jumped in the shower, his cock was still half hard, and he couldn't care less about the few other city workers in the showers who smirked at him.

No panties and a skirt tonight, please. (Max)

Absolutely. (Red)

If you have time over your lunch, edging. (Max)

A photo or it didn't happen. (Max)

Anything you say, Boss. ;) (Red)

He'd show her who was Boss, he chuckled, putting away his phone to focus. *Goddamn, he loved her smart mouth.* It was just so paradoxical to the quiet, calm exterior she often expressed. She radiated with anxiety at times, so he was glad she allowed herself that release, even if it was with a rarely. Maybe he could help her work on that while they were together.

He had some paperwork to wrap up today from this week's investigations. Buck whined at him, reminding him he needed to go out, so he took a break. It had been a long week, with little progress in anything—not his other cases nor the explosion. He'd left a voicemail for his contacts in New York but hadn't heard back from them yet.

Rose had mentioned a Trauma Conference for physicians that she was supposed to attend at the end of next week, but Max wasn't so sure how he felt about their going. Hell no, she wasn't going on her own, especially as it was in San Diego, a beach and close to the border, both risks he wasn't willing to take, at least without him to watch out for her. His boss was willing to allow him to go and work from there for now, especially as there were a few follow-ups he could handle for a recently retired detective on the unit on an old case he had taken over. But Max just didn't have a good feeling about all of it, and he was hoping to hear something concerning his suspicions before then. But the days were ticking by.

(Picture of her sliding the small vibrator down her pants)

Well hello there, Sir, tis lunchtime. (Red)

How long? (Max)

Only a few minutes. (Red)

20 please, but do not come. (Max)

Orgasm control had been on her list, and he definitely didn't mind. He liked to dole them out, and he also liked withholding, as it intensified the next orgasm. She had mentioned a few nights ago that the glue stitches from her scalp injury seemed to be fully healed, and her doctor had agreed at her follow-up appointment yesterday. He did have a thing for hair pulling and figured he did with her, at least, going back to when he was in 3rd grade. His fantasies often involved her long curls wrapped around his hand, so he had been extra careful the last few weeks when he reached out for them.

He noticed the time.

> Did you come? (Max)

> No. Thought about it though... (Red)

> Lol—good girl. We'll see to that later. (Max)

He headed home with Buck shortly after, knowing she was finished with work and they would want to leave for Newheart by 4pm at the latest. When he got home, he walked in and found her bending over to put her boots on, her ass arched and pussy peeking from her short plaid mini skirt as she bent over slightly, already missing her panties. She stood back up, and her plain white business button-up almost hid the red pushup bra she wore beneath that lifted her tits into mouthwatering cleavage.

She walked nonchalantly over to him, her hips swaying that skirt slightly, and she kissed his cheek. Spinning, she walked away from him, drawling, "Just in case you think this might be inappropriate for your Momma and Daddy, cause I do, there is more." She turned to face him as she added a long, fitted jean jacket that came to just above her knees, and she buttoned the next button on her shirt, covering most of the cleavage. The outfit came together like a picture from one of the latest fashion magazines he'd seen at the grocery store had it been Texas style, although he definitely preferred the first option and should have her wear it again sometime for him when they had more time. She'd added green hoops to her ears to match the little red and green skirt that barely covered her ass crack when that jacket was off, and she'd pulled her curls up high in a waterfall of a ponytail.

He wanted to reign in that thick curly tail as he bent her over the kitchen island, pulling up that flirty little schoolgirl skirt and ride her, but he knew they needed to get on the road soon. He changed his clothes quickly, opting for a clean pair of jeans, his own plaid button-up, and his boots. He tucked on his cowboy hat, knowing it would please his father. He didn't hate them. He just didn't love them and rarely wore one. So cumbersome, especially when moving quickly on defense.

But before they left, he pushed her up against the wall and kissed her thoroughly, nearly losing his hat and leaving her breathless. "Don't think I didn't notice that impertinent little ass, Red. It's gonna be mine later." He promised, pleasingly noting how she had clamped her thighs on his leg, leaving a slight wet spot on his jeans.

On the drive, they talked easily about their week, her classes and research, and some of his general investigations. It was so easy with Rose. He didn't have to always have a front turned on. He had to be on top of things all the time. Sometimes, it was tiring. But with her they just flowed. They followed each other's thoughts so well. No relationship had ever felt like Rose did to him.

She talked for a bit about the presentation she was preparing for the conference the next weekend, passionately warning him that she would go with or without him. He knew it mattered a lot to her, so he guessed he would be going, despite his worries. He'd need to make sure his boss followed up with the Chief there. He would definitely be carrying his regulation piece. Maybe they'd offer some backup, although he doubted it.

Once traffic had thinned, he'd rested his palm on her thigh again, as he often did, periodically stroking her soft skin with his thumb. She'd turned her leg to the side and pulled it up a bit in the seat, and he knew she impatiently hoped he might stroke even higher. She'd been waiting all afternoon to come. But he didn't, instead preferring to frustrate her a bit more, raising her libido even higher. As he pulled under the elaborate Anderson Brother's Ranch sign to park in the large garage barn, she turned and straightened her jacket over her short skirt. He felt her disappointment radiate from her with the dark frown and the crease between her eyes. It was then that he slipped his hand beneath her skirt and stroked her wet pussy a few times, knowing he had another moment before they would be seen.

"Mine, Red. At least for now. Whenever, wherever I want it," he said quietly as she whimpered.

They got out, and she did a good job of covering her flush with the warmth of the spring sun as they greeted his mother and oldest brother Nat. Rose didn't generally hide her feelings well, it was one of the thinks he enjoyed about her. Thankfully, he'd left his own shirt untucked to cover the rise he'd had at her wetness. He walked with Nat to the barn for a moment to cool off, hearing some updates about the cattle numbers and staff.

Rose had gone on into the house with his mother and Susie, the part-time house staff they had hired years back when his mother had been recovering from a broken leg after a fall off a horse. She'd stayed on, and no one was sure if it was more for helping his mother or the friendship they'd developed, but she made fantastic biscuits, so no one dared complain.

He checked in on his mare, Shasta, who was aging at 19 years. He offered her a carrot from the feed as she nudged him, remembering her birth as a foal when he was young. He'd later begged his mother to let her be his instead of selling her. He'd tried to get out here monthly since returning stateside to see her and his family, but he knew the barn staff cared well for her when he couldn't.

He headed on up to the house. Nat would check on a few more things with staff before joining them for dinner. He needed to get out to Nat's cabin one day soon and try out the hot tub the brothers had installed a few months back. Nat had been slowly renovating the old cabin that was on the land from their ancestors. It was reportedly the first cabin built on the land back in the 1800's, when the land had been settled by some great-great-great. Nat mentioned that the hot tub had been nice during the cold weather recently. He was just glad the makeshift plumbing the brothers had configured had held up. None of them were actual plumbers. But you could do just about anything with a YouTube video and some perseverance these days.

Jackson still hadn't arrived for the family dinner yet, and Red wasn't in the kitchen with his mom and Susie, who were finishing up preparations for the family meal. So, after stealing a quick taste of the simmering chili, he went on a hunt to find her.

He eventually found her in his lower-level suite, looking at his old sports trophies. No one else was downstairs as far as he was aware, so he decided to take advantage of the moment with her, indulging in an old fantasy. Silently pushing the doorway to his room almost closed, he walked up behind her in the waning light and pressed her against the desk she stood in front of, his hand going over her mouth before she gasped too loudly, his other hand sliding inside her jacket and immediately up her skirt as he gently nipped at her neck. That ponytail had her neck practically screaming for his mouth.

He knew she knew it was him in the darkening room, but he unexpectedly heard his father walk by in the hallway, talking on his cell. Red went still, but he did not, his finger sliding slickly inside her wetness and his palm rubbing roughly against her clit.

"You've been waiting all day. Will my father talking in the hallway stop you from coming now, Red?" he whispered softly in her ear, his palm circling her clit as he added a second finger to her wetness. His hand that was still over her mouth to smother her whimpers was wet with her saliva as she separated her lips to bite his fingers gently in her impatience.

His father continued to discuss the merger of cattle numbers in horribly boring details, moving a bit further down the hall yet close enough that they could still hear him. He wasn't quite ready for Red to come yet, so he removed his hand from her wetness and undid his belt, unzipping his jeans. He wrapped his palm in her ponytail and turned her to kneel in front of him as he let out his cock. Holding her curly ginger mane securely, he leaned over her against the old antique desk and began to silently and slowly fuck her eager mouth.

It had grown dark in the room, but he could still just make out her slim hand sliding beneath her skirt and rubbing against herself as her other hand guided his cock in her mouth, gagging a bit as he pushed in deeper.

"Is this how we keep you happy, my little cum sucking slut? My cock filling your mouth as you play with your sweet little pussy beneath your skirt?" He wasn't sure who enjoyed this more, his 29-year-old Dominant self or his inner randy teenager. He reined in his control, guiding her by the ponytail into his nearby walk-in closet. He quickly rid her of her jacket and pressed her face-first into the far wall as he lifted her skirt and swiftly entered her from behind. He pulled her shirt and bra above her tits so they could rub against the wall while he pressed her against it and fucked her.

His father's voice sounded much further away now, despite the open closet and bedroom doors, and he grunted as he filled her tight cunt, rutting into her as she whimpered and quietly pleaded, "Yes, fucking god, yes..."

One hand against the wall to support herself, he felt her slip her other hand down to her clit to begin to rub. He slipped his hand down to join hers roughly, his hand over hers, knowing he was about to come. He felt her pussy begin to clench and milk his cock as she began to come in the darkness, with a whispered "Yes, yes, yes, yes..." hissing out of her mouth. His other hand came up to cover her mouth, catching her groan in his hand just in time as she went over the edge. He carefully bit her neck—avoiding sucking as her hair was up tonight—to swallow his own groan as he finally came.

FUCK. This closet would never be the same to him again.

He leaned into her against the wall as he felt her sag, holding her up for a moment until he could actually stand. He turned around and held her against him in his arms as he leaned against the wall, soothing her with a "Shhhhhh..." and soft strokes to her pulsating pussy and warm thighs. He felt her breath slowly even out with his and turned her to face him, kissing her softly in the dark.

"We have to stop meeting like this, Rosebud…" he said softly, his hand gently running up and down her back.

He felt her tense. "What—NO," she said quickly. Then relaxed when she felt his silent laughter, not realizing he was teasing at first. She swatted his chest. "Not funny. That was fucking fantastic."

He felt a soft buzz from his phone in his pants pocket, sagging loosely at his hips. Setting her back a bit, he zipped his pants, mentioning quietly that there was an attached bathroom if she needed it. He kissed her forehead as she grabbed her jacket and went to find it as he checked his phone.

Mom's looking for you guys. FYI, she invited Elena to dinner too. (Jax)

Fuck. (Max)

I didn't need to know what the two of you were doing, just get a move on before anyone else questions too much. (Jax)

Shut your hole. (Max)

Lololol (Jax)

Shit. His mother had incessantly tried to set him up with Elena through the years, as she was the daughter of the nearby smaller breeding ranch, the one his Father had tried to purchase over the years and her father refused to sell. The two men had become competitive friends over the years, and while his father probably didn't hold out much hope anymore on Mr. Moreno actually ever selling, his mother hadn't seemed to have forgotten her need to hook the two of them up since high school. Elena had been in his and Matt's class. She had been on the cheerleading squad in high school and at most of his games before he quit, and of course, at all the high school parties.

Honestly, she had seemed about as interested in him as he was in her, but when he returned to Dallas, he had caved and taken her out on a few dates at his mother's insistence. Her now fake-dyed red hair over her previous natural dark brown waves turned him on about as much as her incessant talking. What he did know was that she clearly needed to take over for her father one day. She had a fantastic mind for cattle and numbers. It was all she had talked about when they had gone to dinner. She didn't even really know him well enough to know how much that topic was the least interesting one he could endure, and it had lasted all evening on both nights they had gone to dinner.

He didn't even think she had been disappointed when he hadn't even attempted to kiss her when dropping her off, nor when he hadn't reached out again to schedule another date. *So why did she accept his mother's invitation tonight?*

He pulled Red in for a last brief kiss as she attempted to walk by him into his bedroom. He leaned his forehead against hers. "You go ahead on out. I'll come behind in a few moments," he said, cupping her ass and pulling her into him. "Trust me tonight, okay?" was all he said for now. She looked at him inquisitively in the pale light from the hall but nodded and quietly slipped out of the room.

He stepped through his boyhood room, staring out at the moon that had risen over the huge working ranch outside his large window. He'd had a lot of dreams in this space, many of them of Red, many of them of his future. It felt full circle to have her here, to have fucked her here. He knew more than ever that he wasn't interested in Elena or anyone else his mother might send his way. His veins had been filled with the sweet scent of a rosebud, and he had no interest in consuming anything else but her. He wasn't quite sure how she felt about things, but there was plenty of time for all that.

Chapter 11

Rose

Rose quietly stepped outside Max's bedroom door, seeing no one in the hall. That had definitely been better than her edging alone at lunchtime. She had stood there in the dusk in Max's childhood bedroom before he came in, having just wondered if they might repeat the secretive moments of the weekend before when he'd suddenly been there, leaning into her at the desk, his hand over her mouth to catch any unexpected sounds. She was pretty sure her teenage fantasies hadn't even compared to being on her knees in his childhood bedroom, sucking his cock like that, or being fucked up against the wall in his dark closet.

She'd mostly been able to put herself back together okay, but she had noticed the back of her neck was a little red from the rough scruff of his unshaven face. She liked the idea of him marking her like that, but with her hair up, she wasn't able to hide it as easily, despite the trailing curls of her pony. She was thinking she was going to need to pretend she had been rubbing her neck. Who knows, maybe it would even work.

She slipped quietly past Mr. Anderson's office, his door slightly ajar as he finished his phone call, and silently crept up the stairs back to the main floor. She heard voices in the kitchen and music playing in the background, along with Jackson laughing. She walked in as the older woman she knew helped Mrs. Anderson, patted Jackson's cheeks with flour-dusted hands, leaving handprints as she resoundingly kissed his mouth and told him to finish his onion-cutting job. Another girl around Rose's age, whom she assumed had come with Jackson, laughed and continued to talk to Jackson about his knife skills at the cutting board.

Max must have walked in shortly after her as his mother lit up and exclaimed, "Max, my love, you remember Elena from next door, right?" She beamed between the two of them, clasping her hands together in excitement. Rose suddenly realized that Max was likely being set up by his momma and tried to hide her smile behind her hand. Glancing around, Rose saw Jackson wink at her, catching her smile. Rose quickly looked away—startled that Jackson seemed to read her mind and found it humorous.

Max cleared his throat, "Momma, yes, I know Elena. We went to school together, remember?" He kissed his mother's cheek, side-hugging her briefly. He smiled calmly at Elena across the kitchen island, nodding, "Hey! Nice to see you again. It's been a while."

He was clearly sending Rose a hint that they hadn't dated recently, if they had dated at all. Rose wasn't too worried, as she still ached from being fucked by him in the closet. But now that Mrs. Anderson had mentioned her name, Rose recognized the girl better. She had bottle-red hair instead of the dark brown Rose remembered from high school, but she was still rather pretty, her hair still thick and hanging in long waves. A tad stocky in her petiteness, Rose knew she was an avid rider with her thick muscular thighs in her snug jeans and soft teal sweater that hugged her curves with her black studded cowboy boots. Rose thought she remembered Elena being into girls at one point, having seen her making out frequently with another girl at after-game high school parties. She couldn't remember who the girl was, but it had been years since then.

She offered to help set the table, and Mrs. Anderson patted her hand, telling Elena, "Our Rose has always been such a sweet thing, like a little sister to our boys when she would follow Matthew over here." She took down some bowls and pointed to the silverware drawer. "Susie made her county famous chili today with her homemade cornmeal and cheddar biscuits. You just feel free to set everything up right over there, darlin', and we are going to serve ourselves and take it to the family room, I believe."

In the past, comments like that would have embarrassed Rose, who desperately had not wanted to be seen as a little sister to Max. Today it put her at ease, knowing Mrs. Anderson might not think any better of their disappearing at the same time earlier or the reddish beard burn on the back of her neck if she got too close. So, she just smiled sweetly at Max instead and said, "Yep. Big brother Max is just helping watch out for me lately, as clearly someone wants me dead or something, so I got to come with him tonight." She didn't know what came over her. Her sarcasm didn't usually burst out like that in a crowd. She knew a slight flush splashed across her chest as she realized what she'd incidentally said, hearing Jackson snort into his elbow as he tried to cover it with a cough.

That left Max stepping up and answering questions, explaining how things were going as Susie and his Mom asked for updates. Meanwhile, he nonchalantly pulled out his phone for a moment, typing briefly as he multitasked all too well, and then put it away.

That little girl ass is gonna be over my knee. (Max)

Promise, big brother? (Red)

She slipped her phone back into her pocket, adding glasses for drinks to the items out for dinner. There was a large pitcher of southern sweet tea that had just been made to go with it. Nat walked in, greeting Elena as he washed his hands at the sink. He immediately started into a conversation about her family Ranch and her recent acquisition of a new steer to add to her family's seedstock production.

Mrs. Anderson told everyone they should get their bowls of chili and that they were going to watch an old movie in the family room tonight, so to find a comfortable spot in there. She went to call Mr. Anderson to dinner.

Rose quietly waited for their neighbor to go first, and Nat and Jackson got their bowls of chili as well, moving toward the back of the house. Max nodded his head to her to go before him, so she gathered her things and made her way into the family space, which was much larger than the average family room, taking up the whole length of the back of the house. One side was set up more like a theater, with different soft couches and easy chairs all facing the large screen that lowered from the ceiling. The space was softened by the various plants and large windows surrounding the room on three walls, overlooking the beautiful, majestic ranch, at least four times the size of her grandparents' Ranch. The ground sloped downward from the front of the house to the back and onto the valley so that the main floor at the entrance was the second story in the back, and the lower level was the ground floor for the back of the house, which had always made for fantastic parties.

Rose knew the boys' rooms were all still on the lower level. Nat still lived here on the family property as well, but he had taken over a small cabin that Rose knew was about a ten-minute walk from the main house. Kitty had known how far the walk was once, and Rose couldn't remember ever knowing why. Mr. Anderson's large home office and a smaller entertainment room were down there as well, a place she had been in often as it had been a playroom for the kids growing up, eventually turned gaming room and library of sorts with a big screen television.

Rose carefully picked a spot near Jackson on a loveseat near the back of the room to avoid any awkwardness with the family regarding Max. She set her glass of tea on a coaster on the table beside her seat, and as she got situated, she saw Jackson suddenly get up as Max walked in. Max sat down in Jackson's spot, and Rose quietly pointed out that Jackson had been sitting there.

Max just shrugged his shoulders and said, "Well, now I am. I guess Jax will find another spot," and dismissed any further worries by diving into his chili.

Jackson came back a few minutes later with his drink and rolled his eyes at Max, but didn't even say anything. He just picked up his bowl of chili from the table beside Max and settled himself in a nearby, easy chair.

Elena and Nat were *still* chatting about cattle. Rose wasn't so sure when or if Max had ever dated the girl, but Max wouldn't have been interested in ranch talk for very long. She knew that. She'd heard Elena wanted to take over for her father one day. She wondered why Mrs. Anderson thought she would be a good match for Max because, to her, it was clear she was not. *She really didn't want to think about anyone else being Max's type,* in fact. She stopped that errant thought.

Sitting next to her, she saw him briefly tapping one-handed on his phone.

Yeah. That was never a good fit. Sorry about that, I didn't know Momma was inviting her. (Max)

She's not hurting anything. Maybe even helping distract your Momma from us. (Red)

Momma likes to watch old movies in the dark, Red. Just sayin. (Max)

Rose knew what he was implying. As much as it made her heart race, any sneaking to make out in this room with his family could not even be pulled off without someone noticing. Even if they were sitting on a couch closer to the back wall and his parents were closer to the screen, facing mostly away from them as their chairs twisted.

There is no way, someone's gonna know. (Red)

What does Jackson know btw? (Red)

Jax always thinks he knows shit, but nothing con-firmed. Btw, he thought he knew "things" before anything ever happened. (Max)

Ok (Red)

She had just about finished her chili when Max's father started the old black and white movie, turning off the lights in the large room. The only lights glowed low from the hallway, and the moon shone through the windows. Rose pulled the loose throw blanket that was over the arm of the couch onto her lap, toeing off her boots and pulling her legs up underneath her in a crisscross style.

Max pulled a boot up, crossing his knee. His boot blocked most of the view from others as he gradually slipped his hand beneath the soft, thick blanket. His hand at first slid alongside her hand on the couch beneath the blanket, between them. For a while, as the old black and white movie opened, his little finger hooked snuggly with hers. She didn't know why she thought it to be as sweet as it was, but no one seemed to notice.

Rose couldn't help but think for a moment what it might be like if everyone knew they were seeing each other, or whatever this was. If Mrs. Anderson had thought *she* was a good fit for Max. If the two of them didn't have to hide and she could snuggle up against him while the old movie played and the characters resisted falling in love with one another.

Rose felt his fingertips begin to move, shifting to curve inside the expanse of her thigh, his wrist just settling against the warmth of her. She caught her breath and held it for a moment, but Max didn't move any further. His hand instead just possessively rested there, his thumb periodically stroking the top of her thigh as he watched the movie. Were anyone to glance at them, they would simply see his arm to his elbow at his side, but if they looked closely, they would see that below his elbow was beneath the blanket.

She waited, hardly following the movie, with shallow breaths for someone to look at them and say something. But no one did.

The dark-haired girl in the movie made her declaration of love for the handsome young man who she loved dancing with, and Rose felt his little finger slide to rest along the lips of her vagina. She knew she had to be wet, having sat there for a while now, wondering how far he would take this. But he just rested his little finger along the slit, his thumb continuing his periodic swirls against the skin of her upper thigh.

She noticed the ridge in his jeans and knew he wasn't unaffected. But she also knew his self-discipline was far better than hers, and she seriously just wanted to jump his bones, family there or not. She felt her phone buzz as he tapped out another text with his free hand.

Do you remember that last wild ass sleepover we had here, when I was 16? (Max)

YES. I couldn't believe your parents allowed you guys to have a co-ed sleepover that old. (Red)

We couldn't either. Our Dad found out after that one that we were making out with the girls and put a stop to it. (Max)

You were 13. I fantasized about you crawling into my sleeping bag that night. I was 14, almost 15 and was so pissed at myself. (Max)

> *You were totally making out with Emmalee that night. (Red)*

> *And thinking about you. (Max)*

> *Not just a line, promise. (Max)*

> *I watched you making out with her. That was the hottest but hardest thing ever at 13. (Red)*

> *I didn't want to hurt you. (Max)*

> *Well it did. (Red)*

He softly squeezed her thigh, his thumb stroking what felt apologetically. He slid his hand off her thigh and interlaced his fingers with hers. This was definitely feeling like more than just sleeping together, or exploring shit, or whatever this had started as. She would have never imagined this might be possible between them. It was all she had wanted for so many years, and it had taken her so long to finally convince herself that it never was meant to happen. She didn't know what to do with the softness that was spreading within her toward him.

The movie seemed to be working its way toward the ending, with his mother gushing about the girl's dress in the final dance. Max squeezed her hand again and slipped his hand outside of the blanket and rested it on his boot. God, she felt like they were teenagers all over again and finally doing some of the things she had longed for, but at the same time, she felt a sense of dread, like it could still all be taken away.

Rose yawned as the lights came on. Having pulled her boots back on, she folded the blanket as she stood. Max took her bowl with his to the kitchen as everyone slowly made their way to take care of their things and end the night.

"Maxwell," his father boomed in his gravelly voice from years of cigar smoke. He looked seriously at Max, stroking his short salt-and-pepper beard as he considered. "It was good to see ya again, son. You should stop by the offices sometime when I'm in town, and we'll grab lunch."

Nat jumped in, putting his hand on Max's shoulder, "Maybe I'll swing up there next week. We can make it a guy's lunch. Jax, you can join us." The awkward round of agreement didn't go unnoticed.

Nat walked Elena out to her truck as Max and Rose were leaving with bowls of chili to take home with them. Max's momma kissed both of Rose's cheeks before they left. "Be safe, loves! Trust Max, he has always looked out for you," she said, her kind eyes holding Rose's seriously for a moment before she turned and hugged her son goodbye.

They rode in silence for a while as Max navigated back out onto the old two-lane highway. He reached over for her hand and brought it to his lips, kissing it gently and then tucking it against his thigh as he held it. They drove through town, the already dark windows of the businesses, other than the old boxing gym, spoke to the quiet of a small town. One where everyone knew one another, and almost everything shut down when everyone was settled for the night. Even the small Market on Maine Street shut down at 8pm every night. So much was still the same, yet so much was now so different.

"A lot has changed since we were kids, huh?" Rose asked thoughtfully. They had been so much younger back then. A decade made such a difference, she figured, especially when it was your twenties.

"Yep. You grew up, little rosebud," he said, smiling, knowing she hated being called that.

"So did you," she added quietly. She'd noticed the differences in his relationships with his family some tonight. The brothers were clearly still as thick as thieves. But his parents hadn't seemed to see how much he had grown and changed in the last 10 or so years. His mother setting him up with a woman who was clearly not his type, and the awkwardness between him and his father there at the end, that Nat had saved him from, *what was that?*

"Things were pretty different back then... before I left," he said quietly. "No one was happy with me, especially me. And you were just so young, so innocent..." His voice dropped towards the end. "I couldn't drag you down with me."

She'd wished he had given her a chance back then. Maybe she would have been mature enough. But even as she thought the thought, she knew she hadn't been.

"I'm glad you found what you were looking for," she responded quietly. At 17, almost 18, that wouldn't have been a girl. She knew that too.

It wasn't long before he was waking her when they had arrived home. Well, to his home. He carried her up the stairs, laying her softly in his bed, his eyes gentle as he stroked her cheek, tucking a tendril of her hair behind her ear. Luna came up to check things out and snuggled against her while Max took Buck out briefly.

She must have snoozed a little again as she woke when he gently moved Luna to another part of the large bed. He watched her as he undid his shirt, and she began to slip the top button of her shirt through its hole. He rid himself of his clothes before she had even reached the bottom button, helping ease her skirt down her legs and sliding his palms down her arms to drop her shirt behind her. He joined her in the bed and made drowsy, sweet love to her, the softness between them as vanilla as apple pie.

He slid into her. Drawing her chin down to bring her eyes to his, he cupped her face gently, saying softly, "I always wanted you, Rose. It was always you."

She came so tenderly, the orgasm rolling through her sweetly. He was in her heart, curled around her as she settled, his hand stroking her hair gently until she drifted off to sleep.

Chapter 12

Max

Max considered all the possibilities of telling their families as he finished jogging his second mile with Buck on Tuesday evening. He had no intention of letting her go after all this if she wanted to stay, and he thought she might. It was almost as if life had come full circle for them, only better than they might have ever experienced if they had come together when they were young.

They'd gone on a spring hike Sunday morning and checked off another interest from her list. He'd pulled the small, battery and remote-operated vibrator from his bottom drawer and introduced it to her before they'd left, sliding it into her panties and against her clit, under her tight little shorts. He'd also instructed no sports bra under her little white tank top but had worn one of his flannel shirts until she had gotten too warm—whether from the hiking and warm spring sun or from his unexpected ramping up of the mini vibrator, it hadn't been clear. She'd then tied the flannel around her waist, her chilled or aroused nipples peaked most of the time, the tank top showing shadows of her areolas through the thin material. He'd known her exhibitionistic streak might enjoy the possibility of being seen by other hikers at times with just the tank but within her own control of wearing or not wearing the warmer shirt whenever she wanted to.

He'd played with her in various ways throughout the hike, denying her orgasms at times and enjoying her frustrated impatience. By the time he finally fucked her when he'd pulled down her shorts and sat her on his just-sucked cock at the picnic table overlooking the highest peak, she'd reached her own peak in greater intensity after the day's play and withholding, adding to the orgasm.

They'd have to do that again sometime. He'd rather enjoyed controlling that.

He took the final turn looping back to his condo as the sun was finishing setting. The April sun likely meant some warmth would be moving in, and the air conditioning would start to get a workout. Today had reached the mid 70's. He doubted it would be warm enough to swim on the beach, though, when they headed to San Diego on Thursday evening. Her conference was Friday and Saturday, and while he still didn't have a good feeling about it, he had no evidence to back that up.

He'd finally heard back from his New York connections, and they reported the company had refused to meet with them repeatedly, resisting answering any questions by phone as well. He had found them listed in the brochure for the convention this weekend, however, and that worried him.

Nearing the unit, he noticed an envelope stuck in her car's windshield wiper. Knowing immediately, it had to be related, he took his t-shirt off to handle the envelope from a dry spot. Buck sensed his focus and immediately became alert. He allowed Buck to sniff the envelope, but the sweat on his t-shirt, he suspected, interfered. Buck then sniffed around the car but seemed to find no trail of anything related to the envelope. He hadn't made plans to bring Buck with them to the conference, and now he wished he had. Jax would stop in frequently and even stay at his place most of the time while they were gone to look after the animals. When he traveled with Buck, he usually liked to stay in a pet-friendly bed and breakfast rather than a large hotel where it was more difficult to take him out.

He dropped the letter on the coffee table after he went inside, wiping his forehead with the t-shirt. "That was on your car. Hold on, let me grab some gloves," he told Rose as she anxiously began to reach for it.

We told you to stop. This is a final warning.

His research had told him that the pharmaceutical company was announcing the release of a new medication this weekend at the conference that was being targeted for anxiety specific to trauma experiences. If anything confirmed to him that it was their work, it was this. Why else would the final warning have been now? And how the hell did they get inside the securely gated condo community?

"I know you don't want me to go this weekend," Rose said quietly, "But you don't understand. I can't let someone bully me into stopping this research. Their threats only mean there are more and more reasons why we need to understand how trauma affects us."

"It is just so difficult to control and prevent security breaches when we aren't on our own home turf," he said, frustratingly running his hands through his hair. "I can control and direct so much more from here."

"I know," Rose said quietly, placing her hand gently on his arm. "But you can't control everything."

He knew that. He really did. He looked at her and released his breath. "Okay. We'll go. This feels like a bad decision, though. I won't have Buck. I'll only have my one firearm. San Diego has stated they will back me up if anything happens but won't offer preventative support. You have *got* to stay close to me. You *have* to promise that."

She sighed. He knew he'd made her promise it more than once already. "I will." Rather than argue with him, as he'd kind of hoped she would to get some of this frustrating energy out, she calmly took him by the hand and led him to his bedroom and then the bathroom. Turning the shower on, she began to undress, so he dropped his shorts.

This would work too.

He walked into the shower and stood in the spray for a moment. His head tilted back, he closed his eyes as he allowed the sweat from the run to rinse away. He felt her hand take his flaccid cock and take him in her mouth, his hand going to rest on her hair which was already getting wet as she had kneeled on the tile. He felt himself harden as she took his quickly hardening cock deep, feeling his hips lurch toward her almost of their own accord. He knew she was opening the door for him to control her when he couldn't control his world, but for just a moment, he welcomed the admiration from her mouth, distracting him.

"Mmmmmm... baby, you like a cock in your mouth, don't you?" He knew talking dirty to her escalated her heat.

"God, yes... Sir..." she whispered tentatively around licking him.

"What was that Red? I'm not even sure you know what you said or want. Speak up." He pushed her a little bit, both emotionally and literally, as he backed her toward the tiled shower wall, leaning against it over her.

"Yes, Sir," she said more firmly this time, "I love your cock in my mouth." Her soaked red curls were streaming down her back as she tilted her beautiful face up a bit and opened her mouth to him. He lay his cock on her bottom lip and teased her, sliding in her mouth a bit and then backing out as she closed her lips over him. Much like he would tease her little pussy.

"You like a hard cock in your holes, don't you, Red?" he asked determinedly, not looking for an answer as he teased her again. She'd put interest in a threesome, both with two men and with two women on her list. It wouldn't be a first for him, but it might be a first where he was hesitant to share. He'd been thinking about that one for a bit. Taking her to a few of the clubs he'd worked events at in Dallas had potential.

He wondered if they would be together long enough to explore some of those interests.

"Ride my cock, Red," he commanded.

He led her to the wet stone seat and faced her away from him, straddling his lap. Leaning on his knees, she lowered herself on his cock, her fingertips playing at the base of his balls. Her ass was glorious as she leaned slightly forward, her asshole slightly peeking at him between the thick cheeks as he rubbed his thumb in lazy circles over them. He slid one thumb lazily along her asshole and touched her where their bodies met. She gave a shiver as he passed over her puckered, tight hole. She arched her back a little and moaned, still riding him.

"There are parts of you that know what you want. Do you know what you want, Red?" he grated out between his teeth, knowing he meant so much more than just sex.

Pulling her wet hair tighter at the base of her neck, he slid his thumb to circle lazily at the puckered center of her ass. She began to ride him more wildly, and he pressed his thumb just inside her as she fell apart over him, her tight pussy walls milking his cock as her tiny pink puckered ass clenched the tip of his thumb. Her mewling as she ran her hands up and down her wet, writhing body was beyond his wildest dreams, and he wasn't sure he ever wanted to share this with a club.

God, she was gorgeous. And she was HIS, at least for now.

He pulled her by the hair back onto himself, coming then, pumping into her as she lay back against him in the rainfall, his hands running over her writhing flesh, his mouth suckling her neck.

His.

Rose

Thursday morning dawned bright and early. Rose had packed mostly the night before, and they had no difficulties getting to the airport in traffic with it being so early. Max preferred his own vehicle rather than taking an Uber, so they'd parked in long-term parking, and she knew he'd set up a rental vehicle in San Diego. She supposed his lack of trust for things like ridesharing and not liking the hotel stay as much as his preferred bed and breakfast options were likely fairly normal for his military training. Or his financial upbringing. Max preferred to be in control of his surroundings, knowing they were secure— especially when he wasn't happy about this trip in the first place.

But life had to go on. As it was, she was rearranging her whole life due to this threat, and she refused to be intimidated by some pharmaceutical company that only wanted a fat paycheck in the end over the health and welfare of human beings. *She almost hoped things would come to a head at the damn convention so they could all go on with their lives and research.*

Then she felt guilty for that thought, as she considered those who had been traumatized by their escape from the explosion at the grant funding event a few weeks before. She knew that sometimes she focused so much on logic that she discounted the emotional effects that others experienced, which was ironically her whole focus in the first place.

She rested her head back on the stiff plane seat in business class, still tired from such an early start. No amount of coffee would help at this point, with the sun just starting to rise. The event was starting at 9am today, not that she needed to be there exactly when it started. She didn't speak until tomorrow. She was on a panel of researchers, alongside some names she'd highly valued over the years and respected but never actually met in person. She felt much better about being on a panel discussion than needing to lead a presentation. Social anxiety often caused her fairly intense stress at events like this.

Max placed his hand over hers on the armrest, closing his eyes as he rested as well. His thumb lazily circled hers, and she wished she could curl into him for a nap. But she figured the older gentleman on her other side wouldn't appreciate the display of affection. She put in her earbuds and turned on an audiobook, one she had been struggling to get through lately, so she figured it might put her right to sleep—and wasn't wrong.

She woke with Max's hand squeezing hers repeatedly until she roused. They were just descending into San Diego. Thankfully, he coordinated the rental vehicle, which ended up being a ridiculously expensive Cadillac Escalade for two people who likely weren't going to leave the hotel much. Still, he was able to get them in the vehicle fairly quickly since they didn't even have to wait for luggage, having opted for just carry-ons for a few days.

He navigated their way to the convention center and took advantage of valet parking. They wouldn't be able to check into their room until later. She knew he had called about a room upgrade, preferring a suite versus the small room the convention had set her up with for free. She wouldn't mind the bigger space with both of them there, but she definitely wouldn't have upgraded on her own. She lived fairly modestly, despite the foundation now bringing in enough money that she could live more comfortably. Old habits die hard, and she tended to lean into the philosophy that less is more most of the time.

They'd dressed knowing they would be at the convention today before checking in. They checked their bags with the valet until they accessed their rooms. They had both brought their computer bags with them for now. She wanted more coffee, so they headed to the hotel's chain coffee shop in the lobby. She settled with their things in the sitting area just outside of the shop as he went in for coffee. She was surprised he had gone so far from her already until she realized he could see her from the line he was in. A woman in a suit with a trauma conference badge on settled in a space near her, opening her laptop with coffee in hand and quietly browsing.

"We haven't found the check-in area for the conference yet. Is that on this floor?" Rose quietly asked the woman, nodding her head at the lanyard around her neck.

The woman looked directly at her and studied her for a moment before answering, "The trauma conference check-in is on the 3rd floor." The woman, with her severely tight hairstyle twisted into a knot at the base of her neck, dismissed her as she went back to her browsing. Rose wasn't new to being disregarded as young and not an MD at events like this. She didn't bother the women any further with questions. But she did notice the women's eyes raise and peruse them again when Max walked out with their coffees.

She rolled her eyes at the women's clear interest that had suddenly re-turned. I mean, sure Max was *fine* as could be, but he hadn't given the women a second glance. A shiver slid down her spine at the brief vision that came to mind of what he had just done to her the night before. His hands on her, his mouth. No, for now, Max was *hers*.

Instead of settling near the coffee shop and unpacking their laptops here, they decided to head to the 3rd floor and check into the conference before finding the table set up for her foundation in the presenter and organizations alley.

After checking in and finding her table, she saw the box of items she had pre-shipped to set up the table with had arrived. She unpacked the table, laying out the cloth and setting out brochures, pens, and candy. Not many people tended to stop and talk a great deal at these events. Those interested in funding her foundation preferred to follow up with meetings to review her organizational layout and program more thoroughly. But she did garner some interest now and then.

The day flew by. Rose attended a few presentations to gather information, noting a few things she wrote down for further research. Max was never very far away, especially when she decided to attend the presentation by MidAtlantic Pharmaceuticals. Their chief scientist was a small older man, a bit frazzled in his presentation, excited about new research that she couldn't quite wrap her mind around. Some of it didn't make sense, but he seemed to convince some of the attendees who asked questions without even really answering their questions. She wasn't sure, but she was sure she had heard of Afinaferil before, the new medication they were releasing. She just couldn't remember where.

She knew this little, frazzled old man couldn't do much to harm her, not when she had Max. It was almost laughable.

"Don't take people too lightly," Max warned her that night as she snuggled against him in the fluffy hotel bed. He'd convinced her to sleep naked, although it hadn't taken much convincing. She really needed to upgrade more often. She swore the thread count was almost delicious enough to eat.

But by the time she had finished dressing in her new suit and putting on her makeup the next day, she had pretty much decided that MidAtlantic Pharmaceuticals was harmless. Maybe they just weren't the ones who were threatening her. She didn't want to discount the fact that a small bomb had gone off and put her in the hospital and that multiple others had small injuries that day as well, and things could have been worse.

Settling into her seat on the panel later that day, she shuffled through her notes. She knew Max stood sentry at the door to the room, completely alert and on edge, despite her feeling better about things. If she were wrong, Max would take care of things. She trusted him.

She greeted the other two scientists flanking her at the table, each an important influence on some of the work she had done throughout the years, their interests sparring one another in research and then today on this panel. Further down the table was a well-respected Doctor, long retired but who had begun much of the work they all followed. She knew most were really here to see Dr. Glodin speak, as she was a treasure of wisdom and often didn't make it out to events anymore at her age.

Rose spoke when it was her turn, but nothing that she shared seemed to really be all that life-altering to her, nothing that should have put her life in danger. She answered some questions, one in particular regarding an article she had written a year or so ago regarding health markers and trauma and the co-occurrence with heart disease. She noted that the woman who asked the question looked familiar, but she couldn't quite place her. But she quickly forgot all about it as the room broke into thunderous applause and a standing ovation for Dr. Glodin's work.

Rose thought everything went well and told Max so as they left the room. The lines on his face were tense, and she knew he wouldn't relax until they were home safely. She handed him her suit jacket, telling him she needed to gather her stuff from her table before they could check out, and if he would get that started, she was going to stop into the ladies' bathroom real quick right outside the grand hall where the presenter's table was. He resisted leaving her, but she promised she would be right there, and the sooner they got everything together, the sooner they could head back. He begrudgingly agreed and headed into the grand hall as she ducked into the restroom.

It didn't take her long, and as she was washing her hands, she noticed a woman leaving a nearby stall. Recognizing the woman from the session who had asked her question, she flashed on remembering her from the lobby before the event and then also again in the MidAtlantic Pharmaceutical presentation. Her stomach clenched, remembering her talking to the little old scientist.

This wasn't going to end well, her intuition told her.

Initially, she had thought the woman was leaving the stall to wash her hands, but she walked directly to Rose. She pulled a small handgun out from inside her suit jacket, pushing it into Rose's side.

"Walk quietly outside without making a scene. There is a white van outside the doors to the left. Get in the van," she said quietly but firmly.

"A white van, really?" Rose started... *Could they be more cliche?*

"If you make a scene, not only will I kill you, but I'll kill your pretty boyfriend, too," the woman snarled with a steel smile. "Try me."

Rose knew Max could hold his own if he knew what was happening. But the woman had a gun. *She couldn't lose someone else she loved.*

She'd worry about those feelings later.

She walked out quietly.

Max would be okay. He really would. Maybe she could figure out how to get out of this.

Chapter 13

Max

He saw them go through the side door together. *She would be dead if he didn't move now.*

He used the walkie on his phone to connect with the contact he'd made earlier at their arrival. He moved stealthily, trying to stay far enough behind that they didn't see him. For the first time, he wished he had a more inconspicuous vehicle, as the Escalade was too much not to be noticed. He had worked it out with the local precinct to have an unmarked but tagged vehicle at the local rental agency, so they could track where he went as he followed the white van. Idiots, whoever had assigned such an expensive vehicle. He swore. He knew he likely stuck out like a sore thumb.

He had known something was going to happen. His gut had been screaming at him all day, all week, in fact. He knew he should have just taken control and not allowed her the choice to make some of her own decisions.

No. That wasn't right either. He didn't really value controlling others' freedom, not really. The freedom to choose was what he had fought for. Controlling others didn't give him the assurances he needed, even if sometimes the voice inside him thought it might.

He had seen the woman Rose walked out with and remembered her from the MidAtlantic Pharmaceutical presentation. He had observed her repeatedly in the room as she worked with the old man, his gut telling him even then to watch out for her. Her eyes of steel looked all too familiar, and he swore she might have a military background. Quite the opposite of the little old scattered man, she was methodical and routine and restrictive. He saw her twist Rose's arm behind her back once they were outside, and it was everything he could do not to call out as he followed silently, carefully, waiting for the right time to extract his subject.

He followed them to a nearby warehouse by the water. As he got out of the vehicle, his senses told him they would likely use the water as a route of transportation next. It was much harder to follow via water and not be noticed, but he wasn't new at this. He scanned the area, noting an old aluminum motorboat off the next inlet that he might be able to use, assuming there was gas in the tank.

He slipped silently alongside the warehouse they had taken her in, crouching low and silently pausing. He noticed a broken window where a bit of light shone through. He slipped behind the dumpster near the window at the back of the building. He'd shed his suit jacket, tie, and even the dress shirt by the time he'd exited the car, stripped down to his undershirt and dress pants, along with his holster.

With his gun at his side, he waited and listened.

He couldn't see her, but he could hear a mumbled discussion between a man and a woman, and he could hear noises that sounded like they might have Rose gagged. If that *was* her, he at least knew she was breathing.

"I didn't tell you to kidnap her," came the voice of what he thought might be the older, disorganized scientist from the presentation.

"The opportunity presented itself," the woman's clipped voice continued. "Besides, you want to get this taken care of for good, don't you, old man?"

"There is no reason to hurt anyone," the male voice rushed on pathetically. "I told you that after the bombing! Someone is going to figure us out. We are fortunate that no one has traced it back to us, *and* we are fortunate that no one was seriously hurt! What good does it do for us to help others with trauma if we cause it?" the voice fretted.

"Do you think I care if someone is harmed?" she said dismissively. "I am not the behavior scientist. I am the one they hired to deal with the mess you created. And I *DON'T* get caught."

If she was that confident in not getting caught, she wasn't going to release Rose. Having not been blindfolded, Rose would know too much at this point. His gut clenched.

He had to get her out of there.

ALIVE.

Rose

Rose wasn't sure where they had taken her.

She had gone with them complacently, saving her fight for when she would need it. She couldn't fight against a bullet, she knew that, and her intuition told her the woman had no qualms about shooting her.

She watched the woman and the little old man. If she were going to get sympathy and a possible way out, it would be through him.

She tried again through the gag, "-lee, -lees, I -ee a -ink oh -ater...," she tried to get out, begging for a drink of water. But again, they weren't paying any attention to her. The goddamned rope was cutting into her skin at her wrists.

She tried to at least get their attention from across the room. "-EY!!!" she tried yelling around the gag. The woman's eyes flicked up to her.

The coldness in her eyes was extremely real, and she snarled at Rose in disgust. "Shut up, bitch. You've messed things up enough, don't you think? You should have heeded my warnings."

"Maybe... maybe she needs something?" the older man stuttered, looking at Rose tentatively but then back at the woman quickly. "Maybe we should just see what she wants?"

"Maybe you should shut the hell up with your ideas, old man. It's your fault we are even in this mess. If you hadn't fucked up the first trial of your damn medication, there wouldn't be any questions regarding its upcoming release. Your boss would be happy, money would be flowing, and they wouldn't need me." She looked at him disdainfully. "But now they do. So, we do this my way."

The woman walked over to Rose, looking her up and down. "What a pretty princess." She trailed her leather-gloved fingertip along Rose's jawline as she flinched. "Any other time, I would eat you alive, and you'd enjoy it. But alas, the job comes first."

She backhanded Rose across the cheek, and Rose saw stars. The pain was excruciating. Rose's eyes welled up with tears, but she refused the sob that rose in her throat.

"Think you're strong, Bitch? Try me," the woman sneered with a wink. "Unless you enjoy pain?" Rose quickly shook her head, and she laughed. "I didn't think so. So shut your goddamn mouth. No more! Or there will be more of that."

She lay a long fingertip on the gun she'd holstered. "Or I can just go ahead and kill you," she said, raising an eyebrow.

When Rose's eyes went wide, she smiled. "I didn't think so."

She was probably going to kill her anyways, Rose thought. She hadn't missed the comment about not being caught. The woman made sure they didn't catch her, and that likely meant no witnesses. But if she could keep her from killing her a little longer, maybe she could get the old man to release her or even help her escape.

She didn't know where Max was. She could only imagine how crazed he must feel right now, not knowing what had happened to her. But at least he was safe.

The woman and the old man seemed to be preparing to go somewhere. The woman was packing a large bag. It looked military-issued. What, how? Was she military? Why would the military be involved? No. She said she had been hired. It sounded like a private deal. And she mentioned the old man's boss. So, it *was* related to the big pharmaceutical company. Why was she even surprised? But what had she ever done to get in the way?

And what had the woman said about his ruining a first trial of a medication? She knew she had heard of the medication before, but where... She shook her head as she couldn't remember the name, let alone place it.

The woman put on a rather large backpack and strapped another bag over her shoulder, crossbody style. "Get your stuff, old man. This may take a few days. Maybe a week or two."

"You—you—you mean they might have us stay off-grid until the release??" The older man gaped at the rigid woman. "But I haven't told my wife I would be out of town longer than the conference. She will worry. And if she worries, she will raise hell trying to find me. That's not good, no, that's not good at all..." he fretted, his hands worrying at the edges of his tattered trench coat.

"Call her then." She rolled her eyes at him. "Before we no longer can. See? This is why you don't need anyone in your life. It just slows you down." She shook her head, moving towards Rose. She grasped Rose by the left arm, her arms remaining tied together behind her.

She liked bondage, but not this kind. And this woman was dominant, sure, but she was also uncaring, hateful, and dismissive. She was abusive and harsh. She had no empathy or at least chose not to use it. And that made an aggressive person dangerous.

The woman jerked her towards the long, tall, rolling garage-like doorway on the other side of the empty warehouse. There was a small boat just inside the large door attached to a small dock. The woman pressed a button on the wall, and the rolling doorway opened just high enough that Rose knew the boat was going to be their way out. To where? They hadn't discussed their plans in front of her. The older man had said something about 'off-grid.'

The woman shoved her off the dock and into the boat. Would anyone be able to find her if they left by boat? Where would they go? They were so close to the border, and if they left the States, she would likely be a dead man walking. Well, woman.

The boat was small enough that it rocked heavily, with Rose being deposited in it so roughly. Before she could think it through further, she made a split-second decision and pitched herself against the side of the boat— tumbling head-first into the dark and murky waters below.

Holding her breath, she hadn't thought about her arms being bound behind her. She fought against the ropes, her mouth filling with water around the gag. The ropes were not coming any looser.

She was going to die.

A hand fished her out of the water by her hair. The pain at her scalp was excruciating but was replaced by breath as she inhaled deeply through her nose as water streamed down around her face, and she sputtered and gagged on the dirty water.

She had expected it to be shallow where the dock was, but it hadn't been. She had expected to be able to put her feet beneath her and push to the surface, but there had been no ground beneath her.

And she had forgotten about the damn rope holding her arms immobile.

"Fucking bitch!" the woman sneered. "I should've just let you drown. It would make my life easier in the long run, but we fucking need you in case a ransom is necessary." The woman set her on the edge of the dock for a moment.

"But that wet, pretty little outfit is rather lovely to view now," she wagged her eyebrows depravedly.

Rose had thought the white suit and pale pink corset-style top were fantastic when she bought them. She had reconsidered a million times whether the top was appropriate for the conference, but as her own woman and a business leader, it had made her feel badass. Not so much anymore. She knew the white linen of the skirt was now dingy with the muddy water, and she knew the bodice of the silky, tight shirt was likely see-through at this point. And ruined. Fucking ruined.

She should have worn the boring, tan suit.

Her cold body shivered, wet and gross from the water. Her teeth began to chatter around the gag. The woman looked her up and down suggestively. Her finger trailed down the neckline of the corset, and she pinched Rose's cold, tight nipple roughly, twisting. She laughed even harder when Rose jerked away, almost falling back into the water.

"I'd enjoy time with you," the woman spat out but nodded her head toward the old man without even looking at him. "But that fucker would enjoy it too much." He tried to chatter out a denial, but the woman was right. Rose noticed him adjust his pants. His eyes had gone wide, and he couldn't look away.

"It's your own fault you are freezing and soaking wet, bitch," she sneered, looking Rose up and down again. "Maybe it will teach you a lesson or two, so I don't have to." She pushed Rose into the boat again, this time keeping a hold on Rose's arm after depositing her into the boat. She placed her two bags into the boat and pulled a length of rope out from one of them. She fashioned a collar like a slip rope for an animal. Rose realized it was for her as it was placed over her head.

"If I have to collar you like a dog, maybe this will teach you not to run away," she said, tugging slightly on the loose leash she had created out of the loop. It tugged on Rose's neck, tightening just enough to threaten to choke her if she pulled away. "Now, SIT," she commanded firmly, pushing Rose down into the seat on the boat. "STAY." She snickered to herself but turned back to the gaping older man.

"Get in the damn boat, old man, and don't take all day about it."

And she brought the boat to life.

Max

Max had heard the splash in the water, but Rose must have been pulled from the water before he could figure out what exactly was happening. Knowing she was alive, he went and found the old aluminum fishing boat, knowing they were about to take off.

He hoped the water was busy enough today that he could blend in or stay far enough behind that they didn't notice him.

It wasn't ten minutes later that he saw the boat flash by, going on down the canal, not even noticing him in the narrow inlet off the side. He counted to 10 and then carefully followed, noticing they were flying faster than anyone should go in a busy canal. But that worked in his favor as they were focused forward and not behind them. He could just make out Rose's head over the top of the motor behind their small dinghy. Although he wasn't sure if she was facing forward or back, he was too far away.

He had radioed the team his update just before turning on the little fisherman boat. He made a mental note to replace the boat with a much nicer one, if they survived. The captain had noted his coordinates and checked his cell ping to make sure it was still being received, confirming it was for now. Hopefully, that would give them insight into the direction he moved.

He turned left at the end of the canal to follow them out to open water. Thankfully, the marina was busy, so he could follow a bit closer than he normally would. He clicked, dropping a pin on where he was to show the direction change again whenever a tower might share the signal. They'd moved out of the busier area and southwest, but he slowed down a bit to give them time to get further away so he might not be noticed after he parted with the other boats.

After enough distance, he began to follow again, dropping another pin on the phone. After following even further behind, hoping they hadn't seen him, he noticed a small island coming into view, noting they aimed for that direction. They didn't seem to be changing speeds or directions to try to throw him off course, so he guessed they hadn't noticed him, thanks to the rather small boat he was in. He was about a hundred yards or so from the opposite side of the small island—his goal for mooring discreetly—when the boat sputtered and ran out of gas.

So much for getting out of there. First problem first, he had to get to land. Then he could get to her.

Knowing there was no other choice, he emptied his pockets of everything but his pocket knife. Putting that between his teeth, he dove in. The distance didn't take him long, 10 minutes or so. It had been a few years, but this wasn't his first swim where time mattered. But none of those swims before had mattered as much as this one.

He planned his base tactics while he methodically swam the half-mile, counting his strokes as he neared the shore and his anxiety mounted. She had better be okay.

Thankfully there was a tree line close to shore, and he moved quickly into the trees before he was seen.

The island was small, but the trees were plentiful. Hiding wasn't a problem but finding them might have been if it had not been for the smoke line rising above the small peak to the western end of the island. There wasn't room for too much inhabitation here, so that had to be where they were headed, especially as they had headed in that direction to dock.

Making his way through the brush and looming trees, hearing the calls of the local birds and rustle of small animals, he hardly noticed his wet clothes or the squish of his shoes. He would lay eyes on her before he did anything else. His peripheral took in the details around him, noting the number of trees and sometimes the number of steps between them.

It took him about twenty minutes to reach the edge of the clearing where the small cabin was. His eyes took in his options, and he quickly but silently circled the space and approached the small building from the north, where the trees came closer to the side of the building.

The window was wide open. The woman passed the small open room and was ranting at a young man about airing out the space and how dusty it was. He could see him, barely an adult, poking at the fire in the small fireplace and rolling his eyes at the stern woman. The old man was fretting, wringing his hands as he talked to himself, and he could see Rose sitting in a nearby chair, her hands bound behind her, mouth still gagged, and shivering in her wet, thin clothes.

He clenched his teeth when he saw her bloody lip. It took everything in him not to go flying through that window impulsively, ready to do damage. He would be smart to wait and bide his time. *She was alive. That's what mattered.*

He knew the woman had a gun, and for all he knew, there were more.

He put his hand over his fist at his mouth and let out a low bird call.

Rose

They had been here awhile now. It was getting dark outside, mosquitoes were flying around, and she couldn't even swat them away. She'd die from Lyme disease if they got out of this alive.

She had seen Max, or at least assumed it was him, in the small fishing boat following them. They had sat her facing backward, and she didn't think either of them had looked back even once while headed to the small island. She had known if he had seen them at all, he wouldn't hesitate to rescue her. She also knew he wasn't impulsive and would have a plan. She just needed to wait. Stay alive long enough for him to reach her.

She was cold. So bone achingly cold. And she had to pee.

But at least Astrid hadn't touched her again. Astrid was what the new guy had called the rigid woman. She wasn't ugly. Her hair was pulled back tightly in a style that influenced her sharp jawline, her edges too sharp to ever be considered soft. Her black, thick-framed glasses did little to shield her hardened gaze, and she took in everything, missing very little. She was tall and angular, a little on the thin side. Her dark slacks and suit coat were so simple they could have been bought at any department store. The white shirt beneath was nothing special. But the simplistic outfit added to her no-nonsense demeanor.

Yet her eyes softened a bit for the kid. He seemed a bit young to be mixed up in all of this, but he was clearly some kind of technical genius. Maybe early twenties. Should be in college. She couldn't tell how Astrid and the kid knew each other, but they clearly did.

"Jerome, when I selected you for this job, I did so because you would do it right the first time," Astrid said irritably. "Stop messing with that fire. It's fine. Just do the thing on the computer." She pointed at the laptop the kid had been messing with before getting up to stir the fire.

"It takes time," Jerome mumbled. "You can't download something like that to a server that quickly. I got us in. I got the memory cleared. Now, I replace it. But give it the time it needs if you want it done right." He rolled his eyes, stirring the fire again.

He clearly wasn't afraid of Astrid. He had to be related or mean something to Astrid not to be afraid of her, she thought.

"It had better." You could hear the 'or else' in her tone. "This is our last job, and we can be done. This one will keep us content until we are old and gray." Her eyes flicked to the window as they heard the call of a bird.

"Strange," she said, wandering to the window. "Most of the birds were quieting for the night just a bit ago."

Jerome's computer beeped, drawing her attention back. He shifted to look at it, and she walked over behind his shoulder to watch what he was doing.

Rose knew that low bird call. He didn't dare do it again, but she knew that call. Oh, how she wished Buck were here, but at least she knew Max was out there, and he was trying to let her know he was.

She began to wiggle some in her seat. Just a little at first. If it were their idea, maybe they would trust it more.

She clenched her thighs together a little.

"The girl has to go to the bathroom, I think," sputtered the old man, whom she had learned was Dr. Blaine. He'd been with MidAtlantic Pharmaceuticals since the beginning. He was known for cutting corners, and from what she remembered, had caused a few patient deaths in his last medication debacle that cost his company a major lawsuit settlement. Rose knew who he was, just hadn't known him by appearance until the presentation.

"Let her pee on herself," Astrid stated dismissively.

Dr. Blaine began to wring his hands again, but then Jerome made a face. "That will make this place reek. Now come on, sis."

Rose wiggled in her seat again. Whimpered a little.

Astrid grinned. "I mean, I could give you something to whimper about, little girl," she said, then glanced at her younger brother, clearly deciding to reign in the sexual comments.

"All right," she gave in. "I'll take you, though." She pointed at the computer, "Jerome, keep this baby moving. Old man, I don't trust you with her. You're too soft," she said, as she pushed the older man aside and took Rose by the arm aggressively, pulling her toward the doorway.

It was dark outside, but the woman had a flashlight. It didn't shine very far or wide, but enough to find a space beside the cabin under a tree. The light from the nearby broken window shone out, casting a golden glow over Rose as Astrid stopped her beneath the tree.

"Go ahead. Pee," she snickered, looking at Rose, who hesitated.

Astrid backed up a few steps and leaned against a nearby tree. She watched Rose humorously. "What? Need a toilet, princess? Some of us learn early on to deal with what we have. I bet you've never pee'd in the woods before." She cocked an eyebrow at Rose, who wiggled nervously, tightening her legs.

"Oh wait, need some help with that skirt?" Astrid strode close, her gun in hand as she slid the tip slowly up Rose's leg, raising the skirt past her thigh and up to her waist on one side. She ran her long fingertips suggestively along the lining of the panties at her thigh crease.

"Maybe you need some help with those panties, princess? Hmmmmm? Is that some wetness there?" Her fingertip slid softly across the crease between her vaginal folds. She slapped her hand roughly against her, cupping her. "Are you maybe enjoying this a little bit?"

Rose could feel the gun resting on her hip still. Her breathing was heavy and fast. She knew her nipples were tight and likely still see-through in the partially dried corset. This was oddly erotic— and totally unrealistic. She had fantasies about exploring with women, but not like this.

Max was out there. She knew that. But she also knew he likely wouldn't make any sudden moves with a gun so close to her.

The commanding woman slipped her fingertip into the edge of Rose's panties at the side, hooking her finger and pulling them roughly down her thighs.

Astrid stepped back. "Believe it or not, I prefer my woman to be consenting, not just aroused." She snickered. "Pee, princess."

Before Rose could even begin to think about squatting, she saw Max before Astrid even moved. His hand came down hard on her gun arm, and his other arm came around her throat, clenching tightly as the woman's eyes widened. For a moment Astrid tried to wrestle herself out of his grip, but then her eyes went wide, and she went limp.

"RUN!" he growled, grunting as the unconscious women's body fell back on him, and he lowered her to the ground, grabbing her handgun and tucking it into his waist.

Rose ran desperately toward Max. Rather than stopping to pull her panties up, she just let them finish falling and kicked them off, running alongside him as they ran towards the boat previously docked by the pharmaceutical team. Max didn't waste a second, still moving as he slid his knife cleanly through the rope binding her wrists. When they reached the boat, he quickly did the same to the rope around her mouth and neck.

Kissing her forehead quickly, running a gentle thumb along the imprint of the rope still at her chin, he grimaced. "She's fucking lucky I didn't kill her."

But he turned her quickly back towards the small motorboat and encouraged her to jump in.

"Oh my god," she exclaimed as he moved to the motor to start the boat. "I couldn't believe it when I saw you following in that boat!" Her eyes flew wildly around. "Where is it??"

He grimaced as the motorboat started and then sputtered and died. "It ran out of gas about a half mile out. And fucking SHIT, I think this one is out of goddamned gas too." He glanced up, his eyes going to the cabin. "She won't be out long. I don't know who else is involved and how many more guns there might be..." His hesitation was palpable.

They heard a shout from the direction of the cabin. Jerome had found Astrid and was yelling for Dr. Blaine. From a distance, they heard, "Where is the damn researcher?!"

Rose's eyes went wide. They meant her. *What the hell were they going to do?* Neither boat had gasoline to get out. She wasn't aware of either of the men having a gun, but as soon as Astrid was awake, things were going to get drastically different. She saw Max's eyes calculating a plan. He grabbed her hand and pulled her towards the tree line.

"For now," he said firmly as they moved, "We hide. Until we have a better plan."

Chapter 14

Max

Max didn't know what to do. And he hated not knowing what to do.

He pulled Rose with him, knowing she was freezing cold, still slightly damp from her dump in the muddy canal. The temperature was dropping quickly as well since the sun had gone down. They had to get her warm, or she would have hypothermia. Southern California was warm in the early spring compared to some northern states, but not warm enough.

This part he could manage.

Following closely inside the tree line, they moved from covered space to covered space quickly. Moving them further away from the cabin, he decided not to move too far away from the water. It could be beneficial and a quick way out if the San Diego team found them. At one point on his way in, he thought he had noticed a ledge at the water's edge.

After inspecting it, he realized there was a small cave on the south side of the island, only about 10 feet or so deep, where the water lapped near the edge. He calculated that the tide was at its highest, so they should be safe as it moved out even further in the morning. There were no traces of unusual animals that he could find.

"Go in here, Red. I'm going to gather some things for a fire. You're shivering." His hands rubbed up and down her arms, trying to bring some warmth back in. The moon shone bright enough to cast shadows around them as they stood at the entrance of the small cave. Thankfully, it wasn't cloudy tonight. That made it possible to see in the small cave, as well as possible for helicopters to reach them if they hadn't given up for the night.

Dear God, he hoped they were still looking.

"Hell no," she stated emphatically. "I can help look for fire stuff too. I may not know what I'm doing when starting a fire from scratch, but I grew up on a ranch too. Just tell me what we need."

That was his Red. HIS Red.

"Okay," Max said quickly, moving back towards the tree line. "We need dry branches and sticks. Maybe some dry leaves. Just like your normal fire stuff, really, for now." They gathered supplies quickly, staying together and in the shadows.

They deposited their items on the ground of the cave, where Max quickly began to dig a space for a small fire. It had been a while, but it didn't take him long to start a small trickle of smoke in the kindling they had gathered, blowing gently to feed the slowly developing flame.

He noticed Rose had stripped out of her suit skirt and jacket, shivering in the small shirt that had only partly dried.

"I know it's crazy, but I'd rather stand here naked than in those wet clothes. I cannot stand the feeling of them against my skin for another minute," she said, her teeth chattering together as she waited excitedly for the flame to grow. His undershirt had dried by now, so he stripped it off and handed it to her. Her little shirt did nothing to cover her pantiless state, not that he was complaining, but it definitely added to her chill. She stripped naked without hesitancy and pulled on his t-shirt, letting it fall to her thighs.

She looked good wearing his clothes, just like she had at the hospital. It was hard to believe that it was only just over a month ago. So much had changed since then. He remembered knowing she would be at the event. He remembered wondering what he was thinking, attending with his family when he had spent so many years avoiding her.

Why had he spent so many years avoiding her?

As the little flame grew, he stood back and evaluated its location. He had created the fire pit in far enough that the smoke shouldn't billow in their faces but was also not streaming out the opening. Plus, it was dark, so the smoke was less likely to be seen at night anyways. The flame was well hidden in the cave with them, the opening facing the opposite direction of the cabin, which was well out of sight at this point by the trees and foliage of the island.

He pulled her into his arms and sat with her in his lap, close to the small fire. Rubbing his hands up and down her arms and even her thighs, trying to warm her, not intending to be suggestive. She giggled though and he smiled, knowing where her thoughts were shifting. He blew into his hands and ran them alongside her inner thighs.

"I mean, there is more than one way to warm up," she said. He smiled against her neck.

"There is, huh?" he teased. "You've had experience with this before, have you?" His hands slid inside the v-neck of his undershirt on her, cupping her breasts. He rubbed them more so than teased them, the pebbled nipples likely cold more than responsive. His cock stirred, but he didn't respond to it.

"Well," she started, "Experience, not so much. But you can't deny this...."

She took one of his hands and led it to the apex of her thighs, where she was warm and already getting wet. He cupped her heat as he slipped his middle finger down along the center of her slit. He moved his palm slowly, circling slightly against her clit as she moaned. One hand, still at her other breast, began to gently circle a thumb around the pebbled nipple.

"Astrid touched me a few times tonight," she mumbled out with a moan.

He thought he'd noticed some heat in her eyes when Astrid had cupped her pussy harshly the way she had. "She did, huh?" Gently giving room for her to talk through it, knowing some of it may have been confusing, maybe not. "How did you feel about that?"

"Well, she twisted my nipple earlier tonight after I had thrown myself in the water to try to get away." She thought for a moment. "I don't know that I thought that was a turn-on right away." She had always been very honest and direct. He liked that about her. He twisted her nipple gently between his thumb and forefinger as it pebbled harder.

"See, she didn't do it like that. She did it more painfully, like she wanted me to feel the pain and know it came from her," she said, her breath catching as he did it again slightly harder. "But strangely, it wasn't as creepy to me as Dr. Blaine being turned on by it." She let out a small sigh.

"I bet he would have enjoyed watching the two of you," he said patiently, knowing she had some kink interest there.

"Yeah, maybe." She wrinkled her nose as she glanced up at him. "I would rather you watch."

"I would like to watch," he said simply. This was her story.

"I will totally admit, though, that I got a little wet when she took me out to go to the bathroom. But I can't figure out if it was because I knew you were watching, waiting to pounce or not." She smiled as he slipped his finger inside her now dripping cunt. Most of her skin had warmed up, and she had spread her legs to the fire and the night. His cock was long and hard against her ass through his pants as he played with her, spread wide open to the universe. The stars twinkled outside the mouth of the cave, almost as though they were enjoying the view.

Max had both arms wrapped around her now, his hands at her warm center. One played at her clit as the other slid a second finger deep inside her. She reached up and began to play with her own tits, twisting the nipples harder than he knew she normally did, and he knew she was likely thinking about Astrid. Not one to be very jealous, especially as he had her beauty here in his arms, he enjoyed the view.

As she took the control back into her own hands, she began to moan as he flicked her clit again and again at an ever-increasing pace.

"Fuck, Max, I'm going to come..." she breathed deeply.

"Let it go, baby... come," he said in her ear, biting gently against her neck in the spot he knew turned her on, pulling harder, with more pressure on the hand that had fingers inserted into her, cupping her firmly, as he had seen Astrid do for a moment, and she came all over his fingers, her body bowing away from him momentarily with the orgasm.

Expecting to hold and soothe her, he was surprised when she turned around quickly, pushing him back in the firelight. She unzipped his pants and pulled his hard cock from between the zipper, immediately wrapping her lips around him. Sucking his engorged cock that was already so turned on by her fiery exploration, she crouched between his legs, her fingers of one hand still playing in her own wetness.

She rose, straddling him quickly, her gorgeous red mane flaming in the firelight as she rose above him. She pulled his t-shirt over her head, and like a goddess of the night, she undulated her body over his, her breasts gleaming and begging for his hands as he twisted her nipples to the sound of her moans. She was still soaked, so he slid in and out easily as she rose up to ride him with the stars at her back, the moon shining its approval brightly over her shoulder.

He had never seen anything more beautiful in his life.

When he came—he couldn't have withheld it if he'd tried—he rolled her over and cupped her face, the moonlight in her eyes. "Fuck Red, I love you. I have always loved you. I think I loved you before I even knew I loved you. If anything ever happened to you, I don't know if I could breathe."

She closed her eyes, a happy smile spreading on her lips. "I have loved you since forever, Maxwell Anderson. I think since the first time you tugged on my braids."

His hands filled with her glorious hair and tugged, his final thrust radiating through them both as she came again around his pulsating cock. He watched her tip her head back as he tugged at the base of her scalp, the orgasm hitting her as her eyes rolled back, and she closed them, letting out a deep sigh as it rolled through her, bowing her body against him.

He knew he was heavy, but for a moment, he lay there on top of her, deeply embedded in her warmth, not wanting to lose the connection. He trailed kisses down her jawline and neck, leaning his upper weight on his elbows.

"You are so beautiful, my love," he grated out.

Her lips parted slightly in a contented smile. "I'm glad you think so, Max. Cause I really, really love your cock." And he barked out an unexpected laugh. *Her honesty, dear God, she was so amazing.* Always had been.

He rolled off her, gathering her close, trying to maintain the warmth they'd created in front of the low fire. She yawned.

"Sleep, love," he said quietly. It's not like he would.

But she was already out.

Max

He heard the first sounds of the chopper in the distance just as the faint light of sunrise had begun. He moved to the edge of the cave and saw it in the distance as it moved toward the island. The coast guard helicopter first paused over the old fisherman's boat he could see in the distance, having migrated a bit to the southeast of the island in the gentle waves.

The chopper then moved closer, circling the island until it came closer to where they were, and Max knew they had seen his flagging Rose's white skirt. The chopper moved towards the open beach nearby, and Max moved back into the cave, dousing the remainder of the small fire with sand.

"Red," he called as he finished the fire with wet sand, not intending to bring down an island by fire today. She stirred and mumbled, and he gathered her now-dry clothes. He'd pulled his t-shirt on her at some point in the night, so he moved to begin to pull her skirt on her as well.

"Come on, baby. We're being saved," he chuckled at her grumbly response. "I promise you won't want to miss this."

He helped her to her feet and mentioned the possibility of her pink shirt, as he wasn't sure she would want the rescue team to see her in just the undershirt, thin with her nipples just dark enough to be seen through it. While he enjoyed it, it was up to her who she wanted to see all that.

She waved him away and instead tried to shake some sand out of her hair. "Oh God, I look like a mess. Who really is going to care about the shirt?" She'd lost the hairpins that had held her hair up at some point in the night.

Even now, he thought she was beautiful.

"You won't mind that so much when we get out of here. I promise you a nice hot shower when we return to the mainland," he said, ushering her out of the cave and towards the team of officers and the EMT unloading on the beach. He'd noticed two other helicopters were en route to the island, each approaching from different directions, and he wanted to alert them of the presence of the others on the island.

He coordinated with the police chief, who looked like he hadn't slept last night, to capture the others. He learned that they had finally received the last few pings from his phone at some point in the night when they also noted a satellite signal received from the island from a different IP address as well.

Capturing the other three wasn't difficult. They really didn't put up a fight as there were no further guns involved. Astrid tried to take full responsibility and say her brother, who was just 19, had been coerced into participating. But considering the FBI had accessed the computer upload and downloads, and she had no clue how to explain that, he would likely go down with her in responsibility.

"Dr. Blaine isn't going to survive prison," Red had commented empathetically. The older man's wife had arrived a few hours after they arrived at the precinct, demanding to know why her husband was being held. She had been just as frazzled and a mess as the old man had been.

They stayed one more night at the hotel the conference had been at, courtesy of the elaborate hotel chain, and had been offered one of the honeymoon suites. As lovely as that had been, rest was in order far more than romance. They really appreciated the relaxing jacuzzi tub after a good shower to get the sand out of their hair. The soft bed was heaven after having slept on the dirt ground for the night. Let alone all that Rose had endured prior. Thankfully, all their things had been stored for them, as the police chief had sent a detective to follow up with the hotel chain to secure their belongings.

Jax had insisted on picking them up from the airport after Max filled him in on the last few eventful days. His younger brother looked like he had come from a night of clubbing when he picked them up early Sunday morning from the airport but made excuses about his messy clothes and hair.

"Don't worry about me, bro. I'm just glad you both are okay." His brother's suave tone softened as he held Rose back after a hug for a moment and looked her over. "My rosebud is intact. It's a good thing. Us Anderson brothers would have taken care of things—you know we do," Jax said as he kissed Rose's cheek and hugged her again for a moment.

"The Explorer is at home," he assured Max, "I picked it up from the airport yesterday morning when they called the emergency contact to find out why it hadn't been picked up the night before as scheduled. Scared the shit out of me, y'all! I'm just glad you were back by then when I called."

Jax looked at them both again before he put the vehicle in drive. He liked fast cars, and this little Porsche fit the bill, even if it barely fit their stuff—or Rose in the tiniest of back seats. "You know everyone is going to want to see you both. Momma is already talking about dinner at the house this Saturday. I know you do dinner at the Montgomery Ranch on Fridays. Hope y'all are ready for a million questions." He winked in the rearview mirror at Rose, but Max caught it.

Shit. They had a whole lot of explaining to do. And figuring out what they were actually going to explain.

And Matthew. His gut clenched. *Loyalty meant everything to him.*

But he was *DONE* pretending he wasn't seeing Red.

Chapter 15

Kitty

Kitty saw Nat come into the salon and nervously pace the front waiting area, his tan cowboy hat in hand. His big, towering presence filled the small area more than she wished it did. She tried not to think of Nathan Anderson that way anymore. Her panties had gotten tired of waiting for him a long time ago.

But then she remembered that Kendall had taken the day off, supposedly to consult with a lawyer about how to divorce a man you couldn't find.

Kitty didn't know everything that had been going on with Kendall lately, but she sure knew she wasn't telling Kitty everything... And they had better not lose their salon over it. It had taken her three years to get it to this point, and she was only getting started.

She set aside the broom as she had just finished sweeping up the last trim she had completed. She toed off the electronic vacuum opening in the custom baseboards of the wall that made her life so much easier and wiped her hands on the towel hanging from her gingham black and white half apron. She glanced in the mirror, making sure her hair wasn't completely out of whack—who was she kidding? Her mass of wild curls was always out of control.

She took a steadying breath and turned towards the front.

"Hello, Nathan Anderson. What can I do ya for?" And gulped slightly at the unintended innuendo. She wasn't the kind of girl who stepped onto another girl's shoes, and she'd heard well enough about Elena.

Nat's eyes met hers. She swore she felt a pulse so intense between them. But Nat had never said a word about it. Not since that last time in college anyways. And even then, they had never spoken about that summer they had snuck around in high school.

Not to anyone.

"Hey, Kitty... er—Katherine," Nat said awkwardly. Like he didn't know what she tasted like.

"It's all good, Nat. You know everybody calls me Kitty." She held back an eye roll. There really was no need for this awkwardness between them. It had been, what, almost ten freaking years of avoiding talking to one another around town? Not that she saw him much. Kitty usually tried to be gone to the gym if she knew he was coming in to get a cut, but with Kendall unexpectedly gone today, she had also missed her workout.

The extra energy thrumming in her veins was a killer and did not help the impulse to jump his bones.

"I didn't see you down for today..." she drawled, thumbing through the appointment book at the front counter. The old soda shop counter had been the most fantastic find at the flea market in Dallas when they had gone searching for cool stuff for the salon last year right before they opened. The teal and white, with classic chrome shining down the poles on the sides, established the whole dang look for this place.

And this place was her baby.

"I was scheduled with Kendall," Nat explained, looking a bit confused at the quiet of the salon and not finding his usual stylist ready for him.

"Yeah," Kitty said. "I know she usually cuts your hair. She took the day off unexpectedly, though, had to take care of some personal stuff. I called and canceled her appointments for her, but didn't see your name on here. I'm sorry, Nat." Kitty hated that he had come into town for nothin'.

"Ya know, I'm not a bad cut either," Kitty teased. "I promise I won't ruin those curls." Those glorious curls. She remembered how they felt in her fingers. Please say no, please say no...

"Well, if you're sure..." Nat said cautiously. His hand came to rest on his neck, where the ends were starting to curl up. "I'd just reschedule, but next week is so fuc—er—freaking busy. And it's just getting a bit unruly."

Yeah, she kinda loved when it got a little longer like that on top. There had been more to hold on to. But heaven forbid he get 'unruly.' Nathan Anderson was too done up. He liked to keep things acceptable. She figured she had never been acceptable enough.

She sighed and turned back to the chairs running along the rail facing the wall of mirrors. She knew she looked a little flushed and hoped he'd take that as the early spring warmth from the day.

"Come. Sit," she instructed, pulling the teal chair around so he could sit in it and whipping out her antique embroidered black barber cape to put over him to protect his clothes.

Nat folded his long-ass body into her chrome chair, making it look nearly as small as a child's. She knew he was tall, something like six feet, and halfway towards another foot tall. All she had always known was that he towered over her. His booted foot hooked into the chair rail that ran the wall in front of him as she turned the chair to face the mirror.

Of course, his legs were too long for the chairs. Flashes of his naked legs in her college bed sheets came unbidden. Kitty tucked that away to a place she only pulled out when she was alone.

The hand-woven embroidery at the edge of her barber cape snuggled tightly at his neck, even on the loosest snap. Kitty took out a fresh pair of clean scissors and a comb.

Nat's 3C curls were generally relaxed down to a wider curl like his brothers if he could, she knew. When it was shorter, he was better able to control it. Understanding his hair in a way no other stylist in the area might, Kitty and Kendall were the perfect place for his hair. That was why Kitty had been so irritated when she knew Max was going to that rich place in Dallas. White girls just didn't cut Black or Biracial hair the same. Facts were facts. Plus, they were hometown folk. Loyalty spoke volumes.

And she'd already won their Mama back over.

Her hands shook a little as she ran her fingertips through the thick hair at the back of Nat's head. She forced herself to focus on her breathing and steady her hands. She could do this. He was just the older wrestling champion cowboy she had secretly had sex with a few too many times that no one but the two of them knew about. As far as she knew, anyways. And that last time had been damn near ten years ago. She should have forgotten it by now.

Her eyes met his in the mirror. She felt that pang rush from her heart to between her legs.

Dammit.

Kitty broke eye contact and allowed her usual chatterbox self to rush in and save the day. She tried to think of anything but their past as she began to slowly snip and trim, coaxing his thick curls back into the shape her sister usually cut it. She talked about everything she could think of, from the recent high school football game to missing her workout at the community gym today. It really didn't need to make sense. She didn't care so much about that. She just didn't need any more of the sexual tension that always happened between them to occur while she had sharp scissors in her hands.

And his silence and his piercing eyes were not helping. That sweet heat in his eyes made her want to climb on his lap in the chair, reigning kisses over that beautiful beard.

She was so distracted while cutting his hair that she hardly noticed she was rambling about the tension at the salon lately between her and her sister. Which, of course, led to complaints about the missing lights. Oh, the overhead lights were finished just fine, thank you, the plain ole fluorescents gave the brightness they needed to actually do hair. But there had been specialty lights for the sconces along the walls on both sides that sat with wires hanging out of them, unfinished. Kitty had *really* wanted these cool antique ones that Reggie had promised to get for them in Dallas.

Nat finally spoke up, his eyes focusing in on hers again, but this time with curiosity. "What's going on with the lights?"

"I—" She really shouldn't have said anything. She knew how private Kendall was. They both were, really. Momma had raised them that way.

But the topic also seemed to put things back on a neutral footing for them.

"Reggie," Kitty said, her voice filled with derision for her brother-in-law, "was supposed to get us some lights to replace those sconces. I had wanted these special preorder ones in Dallas. Let's just say we haven't seen him since he took the money to go 'n get 'em." She rolled her eyes but hoped that might be the end of it.

She should have known Nat's big brother shit better.

"Damn, Kitty," Nat's thick eyebrows gathered, thinking. His eyes darted around the room in the mirror. "That's what, 10? 12 lights? Were they pricey?"

Nat's family had money. They were likely the richest family in town, having been here for generations of Andersons, but you would have never known it when you talked to the Anderson brothers. They never talked down to folks. Not that Kitty had ever seen anyway.

"Two thousand..." she barely got out between her tight-lipped grimace. It had nearly been a month's worth of income. They were still building the business. They struggled to make ends meet sometimes, what with the looming business loan payments. Thank God the family home was owned free and clear. It had been in the Mayfield family for generations, although Kendall and Kitty were really the last of the line. Other than her father, who was out there somewhere. That bastard had left them high and dry when she was young, and as far as she was concerned, he was dead to her.

"Holy fuck, Katherine Mayfield!" Nat exclaimed, his eyes building a fire. "That's not okay! How long has that asshole been gone for?" Nat didn't really swear so much, nor get angry, so she knew a fire had been lit under his natural caretaker self. Nat and his brothers had always looked out for the Mayfield girls, just like they had anyone else in their circles. Nat the most. As the eldest brother, he just had that natural-born tendency to feel like he had to protect everyone. And as the lead wrestler on his team back in the day, paired with his height, those muscles tended to work wonders even on sight—before he ever even had to engage in violence. Cause Nat just wasn't naturally violent, Kitty knew. But he'd go to the mat for his people.

And she thought she remembered he and Reggie might have had some complicated wrestling history.

"Yeah, we'll figure it out," Kitty assured him, not wanting him to get involved. "I mean, we are dealing with this whole messed up business account thing on our own. Kendall will crack the mystery before we know it, I'm sure." *WHY had she mentioned that?? Her damn mouth.* She zipped her lips tight as could be, going silent.

"Kitty...?" Nat's voice lowered gravely, using his boot to turn his chair towards her. "What messed up business account thing?"

Kitty turned away, putting her scissors and comb into the homemade barbicide solution on the shallow counter at the wall. She did her best to avoid eye contact in the mirror as she gathered her lather supplies. She focused on her breath for a moment as she mixed and created a good lather with her oils and soaps. Turning back towards him, bowl and brush in hand, she didn't expect his boot to plant itself between her ankles, nearly tripping her into his lap.

He caught her by the forearms as she began to tumble. But he didn't miss a beat when he turned her chin to meet his gaze.

"Katherine Mayfield," he said more firmly. "What did that shithead do to your accounts?"

Struggling to think straight, she pulled back, setting the lathering items on the counter as she turned him back towards the mirror. He wasn't getting a choice in a shave. She gently but firmly gripped his hair—like she had when she would orgasm—and forced his head back in a tilt. His eyes still held hers intensely in the mirror.

She sighed deeply. "I don't know if it's Reggie," she admitted as she began to lather around his beard and neck. "I barely found out there were account issues. Kendall's so damned clammed up about it all. But I trust her with our money. I just don't trust him. She'll figure it out. Maybe. She seems to be avoiding some things, and I can't figure it out. I've searched the account registers but can't find the missing money."

She knew Nat and Kendall had often worked alongside each other in both High School and college when Kendall had gotten that fancy scholarship to the big historic Black university that Nat got into. They had both completed master's degrees in business, even graduating at the same time. They had both always been far better with numbers than Kitty had been. Her brain sometimes struggled to even line the numbers up right in her head, and she could be known to mix them around. That hadn't stopped her from eventually doing some accounting classes though. She knew how to do it, even if it didn't come as naturally to her as it did the two of them.

Nat's eyes were steely as they watched her begin to scrape away at the extra growth around his beard. He waited til she stopped to clean off the lather from the razor before saying, "Kendall has a good head for business." He didn't have to remind her of that. "But sometimes, the heart can get in the way of the head," he added.

Her eyes met his again in the mirror. *Was he talking about Kendall or about the two of them?*

Kitty finished wiping off the remainder of the rosemary lather. He looked good enough to lick. She took a deep breath, letting it out in a final sigh as she wiped her hands on the towel at her waist. She stepped back as she turned his chair, letting him know she was finished.

"We'll figure it out, though. Mayfield women don't take no shit."

Or at least she wouldn't. When it came to Kendall regarding Reggie, she had her doubts.

Nat put some cash on the counter as he stood, turning to her as he put his cowboy hat back on his head.

"No, ma'am, they won't. And I'm gonna help you," Nat stated with a determined glint in his eye.

"And I won't be takin' 'no' for an answer."

Rose

Rose and Max arrived at her family's ranch that Friday, ready for the questions. They'd stopped by the Market on Maine for a bottle of wine and some flowers for her Momma, hoping to soften things. They'd agreed to share their relationship with their families, but Rose knew Max had carried the heavy weight of what might happen with his friendship with her brother all week long.

It was like watching a young, dejected teenage boy who had just lost his best dog, and you just couldn't convince him he would find him. Max was already acting like he had lost Matthew as a friend. She really hoped it didn't come to that. Her brother did have a bit of a temper, mostly because he had a big heart, and he did have a thing for standing up for the underdog. And sometimes, he saw her as the underdog type, which was dumb. His protectiveness of her was too much sometimes, but as they'd gotten older, he'd been able to step back some. Or maybe it was her living on her own away from the ranch. The fact that some people thought autistics couldn't be independent was so disconcerting.

Matt was the first one to meet them as they got out of the Explorer. His hat toppled off backward when he scooped Rose up in his arms and crushed her in a massive hug.

"I don't know what in the hell I would do if anything happened to you, Rosie." She could hear the tears choking his voice. "Dammit, I told myself I had to keep it together." She patted his back awkwardly but reassuringly. He bent over and picked up his hat, slapping it against his thigh. But rather than putting it on, he ran his fingers through his shoulder-length blond curls and looked at Max.

"Buddy, I'm really glad you are okay too, but I owe you so big. You have always looked out for my sister like she was your own." He pulled Max in for a rough hug. "Thank you for finding her."

Clearly, he'd already heard way more about the story than she had told the family. Rose had limited her story with her mother so she didn't frighten her more than she had to. Maybe Max had talked to him already?

Rose slipped her hand into Max's as he drew close to them. Better now than never. Matt glimpsed the connection and looked away but then looked back again. He put his hat on roughly. "I—I—I need to go check the horses. Momma is waiting for you both. Why don't you go on in?"

Rose didn't like the look she saw on his face, and Max tried to stop him, but Matt didn't listen. For now, Rose pulled Max by the hand towards the house. "Let's do one thing at a time, okay?" she reassured Max. "Let him have a minute. There will be plenty of time to talk later."

She knew he continued to worry about Matt, even after her mother caught sight of them from the porch. She noticed their clasped hands and exclaimed, "Well, I knew that one day this might happen!"

Well, that might have been nice to know, Momma. Maybe that would have made things easier before. Rose felt her mother's secure hug. But as they went to enter the home, Max pulled away from her and said, "I can't leave him out there. I have to talk to him. I promise I'll be back," he reassured her. She hadn't wanted him to do this alone, but she knew her mother expected her to come in, and she hadn't seen her grandmother yet either—damn expectations.

She sighed as she watched him head toward the barn, his shoulders squared back like he was facing a military squadron. They had to get past this. She had to make sure they did, but for now, she'd give them some time.

She entered the warm home, her grandmother's tune she was humming carrying from the kitchen stove where she worked. Her old, gnarled hands, twisted with arthritis, stirred something wonderful in a pan. She turned to Rose, her hands reaching to cup her cheeks.

"Ahhhhh my love, it's grateful I am yeez are safe den." The emotion in her voice thickened with a slight Irish brogue that slipped in sometimes when she was especially emotional. She cleared her throat, trying to clear the accent as she normally tried to do, but it continued to slip through. "I am so grateful for that Anderson boy. He 'as always been a strong towerrr watching over ya through the years. When is he going to wisen up to what is rrright in front of 'im?"

Her Momma came up behind her grandmother, resting her hands gently on the older, wise woman's shoulders for a moment. "Grandma doesn't know what I just saw," she said, her voice ringing with a smile. "Rose and Maxwell were holding hands, Momma when they walked to the house."

Her grandmother's eyes lit up. "I knew it'd be so, de starrrs said it long ago." She kissed Rose's cheek and turned back to the stove. She returned to her humming as Rose blushed and again wondered how everyone had felt so very certain about something she had desperately longed for for so long and had convinced herself could never happen.

She sat at the nearby kitchen table, her hands worrying at the hem of her jean jacket. She couldn't help but wonder what was happening out at the barn. She wanted to fix things for them, but she knew she couldn't.

Her Mother stopped at the table beside her, carrying plates and silverware. She set it all down and for a moment, slid a thumb across the worry lines between Rose's brow, tipping her chin up to look at her.

"They will work things out, love," her mother assured her. "People who love each other usually do. Sometimes it just takes time."

*(***TW: suicidality, eating disorder***)*

Max

Max had walked through the doors of the barn, noticing Matt slamming things around as he fed and settled the house horses for the night. He silently joined in, topping off the water in the small troughs in each stall as his friend slammed his pitchfork into the hay bales and offered fresh hay to the horses for the night.

They worked quietly. Matt's anger was palpable for a good 15 minutes before he initiated the standoff that Max had expected.

"My sister, Max?" Matthew's angry tone exploded, his hands balling into fists at his side as his feet planted firmly on the ground in a fighter's stance.

"Why *my* sister? You could have literally almost anyone in the world, but *my sister*??"

Max had known this was coming. That confrontational stance was how he had first met his best friend, taking a brawler's stance on the playground against the bullies. Matt would always fight for what he felt was just. Angered by the bitter taste of things that felt wrong. He knew that's what his friend had struggled with, especially more recently being a police officer before retiring to focus on the ranch.

But Max wouldn't hit Matt. He refused. If anything, he deserved a few from his friend.

"I know…" he began cautiously, begrudgingly. "But what you don't know is that I love her, Matt. I think I have loved her since I was 16 and began to notice she was more than just a kid sister."

The bloody lip that followed was expected. A clip to the jaw was Matt's usual first offense position. Max deserved that. If Matt only knew the teenage fantasies he'd had about his kid sister, he would get far worse than that.

He planted his feet, but he kept his hands from balling up. He absolutely refused to hit his best friend.

"Put your fucking hands up, you bastard!" Matt's teeth clenched fiercely. He wanted a fight, but Max was not going to give him one. He tucked his hands in his pant pockets intentionally.

"You can hit me all you want, but it doesn't change my love for her," he said quietly but firmly. He knew it was 14 steps to the door, but he wasn't leaving. "She and I seem to have avoided one another for over ten years. Wasted time, man. She loves me too, and this will not go away just for some protective guardian stunt you or I have towards her."

"Well, of course she loves you," Matt spat. "She always did. But you didn't pick her up off the dirty ground in this very barn after she passed out trying to hang herself from the rafters long after you disappeared, and she couldn't get past her love for you. You didn't watch her wither in a hospital because she refused to eat in her depression or move on from thinking about you. It took her a full year of intense therapy before she began to show signs of being herself again."

Max felt like he'd been punched in the gut, nausea flooding him as he clenched his jaw. There were ten rafters overhead, one near the barn loft. Was that where... the reality of the past slammed him in the face like a brick wall. "I didn't know... I just—I didn't know..."

Guilt slammed into him like a racehorse. His head clouded with incriminating voices. Was he doing the right thing? Maybe he should stop things where they were. She—she might have died because of him...

"Of *course,* you didn't know," Matthew continued, his voice lowering slightly as some of the anger depleted, and Max heard some of the sadness. "I thought I was protecting you from that. I knew she had a crush on you, man, but I thought you never knew. I thought I was protecting you from that goddamned guilt you carry over you like a dark cloud all the time."

Matt ran his hand through his golden-tipped curls, scratching his bearded chin. "I mean, it's not like you did anything to lead her on..." He looked at Max, searching for the answer to whether or not he had.

Max turned away, walking to the doorway and standing there to stare at the sunset on the edge of the fields. "I did, though, Matt," his voice dropped as he let out a regretful sigh. "We—we—had a moment the night of her 16th birthday. I backed out. I didn't want to hurt her. I left... *I left her...*" his incriminating voice rumbled through him, biting back tears as he thought of a teenage Rose and how hard things had been for her, so much more than the heaviness he'd carried, even then.

Matt came to stand beside him, considering the horizon as well. He let out a heavy sigh after a few moments and said, "So, you tried to protect her then."

Matt roughly ran a hand through his blond curls again, seeming to release something into the night air. "Max, her difficulties then were about so much more than you. You were just the final catalyst." He glanced over at Max. "Between our dad dying and her life changing so drastically when she was young... You know Rose is different. She deals with things differently than most folks. Change is extra hard on her. But I learned long ago that I had to stop trying to fix things for her."

He turned to Max. "She's stronger than most of us think. Don't you take advantage of her." His tone seemed to offer a begrudging acceptance.

Max turned towards his friend, the third brother of his youth that the universe had offered him. Embracing him briefly, he said, "I would never take advantage of her man. I guarantee you that. She's had my heart longer than I even knew." He swallowed his doubts about himself and her past that he'd never known until now. He'd explore that more later.

"Just, you're gonna have to give me a little time on seeing the lovey stuff between you two," Matt said with a grimace. "It kinda makes me want to pop you in the nose."

But he slung his arm around Max's shoulders, and they started to walk towards the house. "Come on, Momma's got a roast on tonight."

Chapter 16

Max

His momma had been genuinely surprised but fully accepting, even delighted by the news of their getting together. His brothers hadn't been surprised at all, and strangely neither had his father. From what he could gather, especially without sharing her story that wasn't his to share, everyone seemed aware that Rose had crushed on him in their teen years, but no one seemed aware that she had struggled as much as she had her junior year. He suspected the Montgomery family had kept things quiet to protect her when she had been in the hospital.

He hadn't told Rose he knew yet. He'd been thinking it all over since the weekend, trying to figure out if there was something here he should do differently and if there was a reason for them not to continue. But generally, he came back to the fact that they were much older now and that no one had the right to decide for Rose but Rose.

Not even him, no matter how much he cared for or wanted to protect her. But he hadn't brought it up yet, either. And it had been a week. A week where he just wanted the softness between them to last, and his constant underlying fear was that it wouldn't.

She was warm and naked, snuggling against his side on this early Saturday morning. He had woken early like he usually did, and he knew Buck would be up for their usual run. Faint light was just coming over the horizon and shone through the window softly on her cheek.

He couldn't imagine life without her in it. Not now, not ever. But she almost hadn't been alive to be here. His stomach rolled again with the information he had held close to his chest now for a week. He knew keeping it from her wouldn't end well.

But he let her sleep as he slipped his arm slowly out from beneath her. Pulling on jogging pants and grabbing socks, he headed out on the road with Buck.

The slap of his feet on the concrete tracked the counting of his steps as they always did. Buck looked back at him periodically as if he could sense the heaviness he carried. He pushed them both an extra mile today, hoping the exhaustion might turn off his brain, knowing it likely wouldn't.

After returning, feeding Buck and greeting Luna, who rubbed sweetly against his leg, he took a quick shower. He wrapped the towel around his waist, leaving the bathroom to find her languishing in the bed, her legs spread invitingly as she played with her nipples.

He raised an eyebrow and leaned casually against the bathroom doorframe for a moment.

"Everyone should get the opportunity to start their day with something so sweet," he said. Dropping his towel as he crawled onto the bed, hands sliding up her legs as they spread even further with him between them. He found her core and used the tip of his tongue to flick teasingly against her wet slit.

She continued to play with her nipples as her eyes turned molten with his touch, wiggling impatiently against the pressure of his hands on her thighs.

"If I have to be awake before 10, at least make it worth my while," she drawled in a sleepy but sexy voice, her ginger curls tousled around her head and over her shoulders like a cloud.

He smiled against her soft skin as he hitched her legs over his shoulders, his fingers joining his tongue as he found what made her squirm. Her moans rolled over him, and her restlessness against his firm hold on her thighs and hips made it apparent that she had woken in quite a mood.

When he finally flipped her over, pulling her ass up high as his cock entered her wet, warm sweetness, she had already come once and was riding high on sensitivity. He knew his cock against her clitoris was overly sensitive, so he gathered her hair and pulled gently to balance the sensations.

An image flitted through his mind from when he was a young cowboy, and he had thought about how good it would be to ride her this way.

He hadn't had a clue how good it would be between them. He had known *NOTHING*. At almost 30 she was far more beautiful, intelligent, and inspiring than she had even come close to being when she was a teenager.

He leaned over her, his mouth near her ear, his other hand sliding around her to pinch lightly at her nipple.

"I imagined fucking you in all kinds of ways, every day, as a young boy, but none of it could have compared to you now," he growled in her ear.

"You are so fucking mine, every inch, every taste, every time," he said, his teeth catching her ear as he tugged her hair a little harder. "Your pussy is *MINE*, do you understand that? I will take it whenever and wherever I want." He slammed into her. "And I am yours."

And they came together—mind, body, and soul, as one.

Rose

She curled into him, back to his front, as she caught her breath. Max ran soothing hands slowly over her. Then idly, just a fingertip, up and down her side.

She'd known something had been off since they last went to her parents. She figured it had been the tension between Max and Matt, but they seemed to have repaired it somehow by the end, and she knew they had texted some throughout the week. So she had kept waiting for him to bring whatever it was up, and he hadn't.

She knew that things were okay enough between her and Max, or they wouldn't have connected so intensely this morning.

But she was tired of waiting.

She pushed him over on his back, straddling him.

"Ready again already, huh? That was a fast recovery," Max chuckled, and she felt him stir a bit against the crack of her ass as she settled at his waist.

"Nope," she said, removing his hands that had strayed to her breasts and sliding them down to her waist instead.

"I know something has been wrong for a while, Maxwell Anderson. Since you talked to Matt the other day," she said simply. "Out with it."

He looked from her face to her nipples. "You want to talk about this now, like this?" He gently rubbed his thumbs against her hips.

She took his hands and held them together over his head against the pillow, bringing her face down closer to his. Smiling with her kiss, she said against his lips, "There will always be this between us. But there is something else that is between us, and I want to know what it is."

He nipped at her lower lip, slightly arching his hips so his hardening cock slid along her ass. He let her hold his hands there momentarily and then easily broke loose, capturing her hands to bring them to his chest.

"Okay," he said. "But this is serious stuff," he added, his face growing more solemn.

He turned her on her side, and they lay face to face. He tucked a wild curl behind her ear.

"When Matt and I talked the last time we were at your parents," he said hesitantly, "he told me about things getting pretty bad your junior year." He watched her closely.

She swallowed. *FUCK.* She'd known he probably eventually needed to know about that, but *FUCK.*

She searched his gaze. There didn't seem to be any disappointment, judgment, or retreat. Most of all, she had been afraid he would pull back and disconnect from her when he knew.

She stared at her hands that were still in his, and she gave a half-hearted attempt to wriggle them free. He kept them gently but securely captured in his, against his chest. He didn't force her eye contact, but he did maintain that connection between them, softly kissing her forehead.

"I..." Rose began hesitantly, "I had been struggling long before that."

She ducked her head, turning to look outside the window. The sun was shining fully, and Texas in the spring was beautiful. She knew the grass would be greener today than it had been last week. Recent rains would have helped. There would be buds on the trees.

"It got really dark in my head for a while after you left. For a little while, I thought it was mostly about you. I had loved you for so long already at that point. But I think you were often just a way for me to distract myself from my grief, you know?" She glanced up at him, his eyes compassionate and listening.

He had always listened to her.

The words got stuck within her for a moment before she continued, but Max just waited patiently.

"I mean, don't get me wrong, you were the hottest thing I had ever known." She shyly smiled into his eyes and glanced back out the window. "But my dad's cancer, and then his death, and then moving—new people, new places, new routines, even new sensory input. It had all just been too much." She sighed. "And I never felt like I fit in anywhere—except sometimes when I was with you and Matt. You always made me feel like I belonged, even if I was weird—when I dared come out from behind my books."

"That year just felt so alone, so empty," she continued, "Kitty knew I'd had a crush on you, but she was unusually busy that summer working, so I never even told her about that night after my birthday. Matt had gone off to college in Houston. Sure, he came home some weekends for Momma's cooking and laundry. But the house was always so quiet, and Papaw had started to get sick. I know I'm the reason Matt came home—after he was the one who found me and I was in the hospital for three long months. I felt so guilty for that for so long that he didn't get to stay and be free in Houston— like I had stolen his future from him. But honestly, it's what helped me get past you enough, I think- knowing I wouldn't have wanted to hold you back too." She looked at him again, a solitary tear trickling from her eyes.

"I'm not gonna lie—it was a hard year. The depression was so heavy, I just stopped talking again, like I did when I was little," she said, voice dropping to a whisper. "I stopped eating. I just wasn't hungry, ever. They put a feeding tube in me for a month before I finally started to eat again— slowly, surely."

"I just lost a reason to be alive, I think," Rose said softly, barely a whisper.

"But one day, there was a new therapist," her voice picked up a bit. "She brought her therapy dog and art supplies. She didn't try to make me talk. She just turned on some jazz music and began to paint. Eventually, Dakota—that was her dog—sniffed my hand, and I pet him. He was the first living thing I had been willing to touch in months. He quietly snuck his way into my heart, and eventually, so did the therapist. I painted with her and gradually began to see the colors of my world again. I also learned that my autistic brain is different from many other people, and I express myself differently sometimes. I understand things differently sometimes too, and that it's okay just to be me in my own way. Learning to accept myself became the doorway to accepting the grief in my life. I didn't need to change things anymore. They just were what they were—all the differences and loss and heartbreak—all of it."

He stroked another curl behind her ear as she turned back towards him from looking out the window. "I was afraid to tell you, afraid you might think I was too weak to stay," she said in barely a whisper.

He took her chin and turned it up towards him, peering into her eyes for the moment she could handle. "Rose Montgomery, you are one of the strongest people I know—you always have been," he said quietly but firmly. His hand stroked her hair down the back of her head, coming to rest on the curve of her neck.

"You know my brain is different too, in the way it counts and tracks everything, seeks to control things and all," he reminded her gently, knowing as a young teen she had been the only one who knew. When she nodded, he continued.

"You and I, we have always understood each other." He stopped and chuckled, "Well, all except the attraction part when we were younger, I guess, but even that, we are on the same page now."

"I know you, Red," he said firmly. "I love you, every part of you—even your past, especially your past." He grimaced as he pulled her close. "I am just so sorry I wasn't there for you."

"Honestly," Rose said, "I don't know that I would have resolved every-thing had we had all this back then." She innocently slid her hand down his body, making his cock jump, and he smiled.

"I don't know that either of us would have accomplished all we had if we hadn't been able to part ways and grow up," she finished, nipping his lower lip.

His hand slid down with hers and held her hand to his hardening body.

"No need to stop now on my account," he laughed. "I'm not going anywhere, Rosebud. Where you are, I will always be from now on."

"Anything else we will accomplish together," he said, dipping his head to capture her mouth.

More stories ahead from Newheart, Texas! Like what you saw about Kitty and Nat? That one is next!

Keep your eye out, and rope 'em in!

Aisling Storm writes emotional, imaginative romance for hearts that crave both heat and healing. She's as passionate about writing as she is about thunderstorms, twin moons, and antique treasure hunts. She lives in the city with her found fur-family, and a belief that love will always find a way.